A LOVE APART

A LOVE APART

a novel

Rachelle Rogers

InWordBound
press

Asheville, North Carolina

For those who've come back
to do it differently

Acknowledgements

I want to thank the members of my original Asheville writer's group—Tamara Ball, Alice Johnson, Wendy Kirkland, Virginia McCullough and Peggy Millin, whose perception, insight, and encouragement helped shape this novel. I am also deeply grateful to my Wildacres Writers' Workshop creative family for nine summers of generously and lovingly inspiring both my craft and my spirit.

Long Years apart—can make no
Breach a second cannot fill—
The absence of the Witch does not
Invalidate the spell—

The embers of a Thousand Years
Uncovered by the Hand
That fondled them when they were Fire
Will stir and understand—

—Emily Dickinson

CHAPTER 1

We wake from one dream into another dream.

—Ralph Waldo Emerson

The young nun lay curled on a cot inside the cold, stale air of the convent walls, weeping. Coarse linen pricked her tender skin, skin that had once known the softest silk. Around her neck a crucifix reminded her of both responsibility and impiety, of a passion she could not put to rest. Always, he haunted her visions and heart. The beautiful man turned monk. Lover. Husband. How he'd made her feel alive in ways she couldn't have imagined, ways she would never know again. Over and over she reached toward him. Always he remained on the other side of an invisible yet impenetrable barrier that condemned her to restless, inconsolable nights.

Lily awoke sobbing. Her body trembled with a frightening desire. She reached for a tissue, then lay back waiting for the feelings, which were not her own, to subside. Through the partially opened blinds, a bright moon lit the pre-dawn sky. In the distance, Lily could hear the crunch of tires on gravel. Someone is out early, she thought. Or home late. Maybe there were other dream-stalked insomniacs wandering the wee hours. Maybe they should form a therapy group, arrange to meet at some all night diner to dissect their plaguing visions. Lily traced the sound of the car until it disappeared somewhere along the quarter mile curve of forest below, then closed her eyes.

For weeks she'd been dreaming this nun and monk from what seemed to be another time, centuries before. At first, the dream was remote, surreal. She hovered above it, viewed it like a film. But then, as the vision repeated itself with growing intensity, the emotional distance between Lily and the young nun narrowed until there was hardly any separation. Often, a feeling of disorientation lingered through Lily's waking day, disrupting the balance she'd managed to sustain within her own heart.

In her real life, Lily was finished with all-consuming passion. The one time, fourteen years before, when she'd allowed herself to feel that deeply for someone, it had led to heartbreak and disappointment. She'd met Alex when she was twenty-eight, working as a copy editor in New York City. Intelligent and sensitive, Alex spoke to her of high ideals in relationship. Compassion, communication, honesty. They fell deeply in love, made plans for a life together.

But despite his fancy talk, when it came the most important time for it, Alex couldn't tell Lily the truth. She had to find out from a friend that he'd been seeing other women. When Lily confronted him, all Alex could say was he was sorry, he'd done his best, he wasn't ready to settle down...which, to Lily, meant the love he'd professed to have for her had been nothing but a lie.

Devastated, Lily had vowed never again to open herself to that kind of emotional pain. Soon afterwards, pretending she was beyond passion, Lily settled for less and married Michael. Nine years later, that too ended and she moved forward on her own. Now, she had her bookstore, InWord Bound, to run, poems to write, flowers to grow. What more did she need?

Unable to fall back to sleep, Lily slipped on a robe and meandered toward the kitchen to make a cup of tea. She was tired, and every cell of her felt unsettled. She wondered if she might be heading for some kind of breakdown. In the dream, Lily *was* the young nun. Lily *saw* the vision of her monk, his black curls and blue eyes, *felt* the nun's overwhelming grief, and anger, and longing. And yet she had no context in which to understand any of it.

What was she doing dreaming about nuns and crucifixes anyway? Lily wasn't even Catholic. She came from a family she, as a teenager, had called "pseudo-Jews," practitioners of tradition devoid of spirituality. And only if it didn't interfere with contemporary indulgences. When the World Series happened to coincide with Yom Kippur, the highest holy day of the year, religion took a back seat to the New York Yankees.

Although Lily's parents hadn't exactly worshipped the God of the Old Testament, neither had they questioned Him. On occasion, they sited biblical transgressions in an attempt to deter their daughter from behavior that might cause gossip among the neighbors. "I don't want you in Herby's apartment when his parents aren't home!" her father would shout. "Do you want all the yentas on the second floor to think you're some kind of Jezebel?"

To Lily, however, it had seemed more reasonable to believe in nothing, than in a vengeful deity who sat in judgment of those who were in any way enjoying themselves. She grew into adulthood feeling isolated and lonely, a mere mortal on a finite journey whose course was set by circumstances beyond individual control. A journey she supposed ultimately led to the annihilation of the physical body and the snuffing out of consciousness. Yet, a faint echo from the caverns of her deepest self often whispered this might not be the case.

Craving something sweet, Lily uncovered a plate of chocolate chunk cookies she'd baked the day before. She didn't count calories. Small boned and slender, she sometimes worried about becoming too skinny, a look she thought unattractive. Lily carried the tea and cookies onto the patio. She stretched out in a lounge chair. To the west, the almost full moon was still visible through the lacy shadow of new leaves. To the east, the Blue Ridge mountains would soon take shape against a blush of North Carolina morning. It was the time of year when everything hummed with the latent promise of summer. But Lily gave little of her usual attention to the imposing insect chorus that swelled the air, or the sweet waft of night-blooming jasmine that rode in on a thin breeze. She was still preoccupied with an inner landscape.

Like she'd done as a child, Lily hooked her finger around a tuft of short, now copper-streaked hair, twirling it over and over. *Celeste.* She hadn't thought that name in eons. Suddenly, she re-visioned her five-year-old self alone in bed at that dark hour right before sleep when apartment windows creaked, and the radiator sputtered, and that one bulge in the old plaster wall shaped itself into the shoulder of a giant who could slip into her dreams. She recalled how, when she awoke frightened, Celeste, her own angel, had come to comfort her. She'd materialized in an iridescent flutter of butterflies that came to rest, like a living bonnet, in Celeste's golden hair.

Lily smiled at the memory of her childhood companion. She reached for another cookie. Although coffee and black tea made her jittery, chocolate, for some reason, calmed her. *Where are you now, Celeste? Can you light the shadows of my grown-up dreams?* Lily sent her questions silently into the night, half-heartedly, almost mockingly, her forty-two-year-old self no longer believing they would be answered. She reached for the soft woolen throw nestled near her feet, drew it around her to protect against the chill of mystery. She gazed across the gentle slope of hill before her. The softening shadows of trees and meadow soothed her.

For weeks, Lily had recorded the dreams in her journal, but spoke of them to no one. Now, in the last hours of yet another sleepless night, the presence of the young nun still so immediate, Lily wondered just what was real and what wasn't. Too comfortable in her cushy lounge chair, she caught herself about to doze off. If she fell back to sleep, she'd never get up in time for work. She gulped the last of her cold ginger tea. It made her shiver. Some philosophies proclaimed everything to be illusion. Was reality that insubstantial? Lily hoped not.

As if to reassure her, the song of a Carolina wren accompanied the first pale ray of daybreak. It seemed to be calling *Steeyoueee Steeyouee*. It made her smile. Lily couldn't imagine a world without beauty. She turned toward the graceful shadows of daffodils and tulips in bloom beside the patio, their daytime colors soon to awaken with the sun. She gazed across the cloudless expanse of violet sky. Points of light still shimmered, mostly a ghostly graveyard of stars, yet to the eye wondrous and real.

There are some illusions, Lily thought, I'm not yet ready to dispel.

CHAPTER 2

*The artist is a receptacle for emotions that come
from all over the place: from the sky, from the earth,
from a scrap of paper, from a passing shape, from
a spider's web.*

—Pablo Picasso

Julian shifted restlessly in his bed poking angles of himself up through the covers. He was not yet used to the nightly haunting of owls and roar of cicadas, which disturbed him more than the New York City traffic had below his upper west side apartment. When Sam was alive, New York had seemed the ideal place to live. Museums, theater, ballet, great restaurants, good friends—together they'd shared these things for seven years. "He was remarkable," Julian heard himself say so often in the last ten months. "Even when the cancer had gotten the best of Sam's body," Julian would explain, "he never let it destroy his spirit."

Julian had loved no one more than Sam, and the

emptiness became too heavy to hold. Everywhere he turned, Sam was missing. He was missing from the breakfast table with his dark, tousled hair and soulful eyes, attempting to smile through the remnants of a late evening of champagne and museum fundraising. He was missing from Julian's bed when he reached for him in the slant of night. He was missing in a vacant toothbrush slot, the glaring order of a desk, the ten thousand things that wore his imprint in a home and in a life.

For weeks after Sam's cremation, Julian had eaten meals out, and more often than not, had let himself fall asleep on the living room sofa, where he'd remained until morning. The memory of Sam's frail and unconscious body, the same body that had once navigated the slopes of Aspen, filled Julian with impossible grief. Over and over, he re-lived those last hours by his lover's side, his hand wrapped around Sam's bony fingers, struggling to let him go. Three months later, he carried his ashes all the way to Paris.

Little by little, Julian came to see he did not know himself apart from their relationship. Even his art, he admitted, wasn't pure, but had often been calculated to please his lover. Not that it had to. But Sam was a curator for the Museum of Modern Art and himself a fine painter, and what Sam thought of Julian's work mattered to Julian. Perhaps too much, and the feeling of being estranged from his own authenticity tugged at him.

Why am I so afraid to look inside my own skin? Julian had caught himself thinking in a courageous moment. But too distraught to search further, he'd drowned his questions in the cacophony of a busy life.

Hiding his pain beneath a spurious façade, he appeared solid as Da Vinci, when, slippery as Dali, he was dripping over his own edges. With Sam gone, there was no longer anyone to anchor him, nor anything to root him to a surreal city filled with ghostly memories. He needed something primal, something with presence and permanence, and the ancient hills and peaks of the North Carolina Blue Ridge called to him. As a child he'd spent happy summers in Asheville. In an inexplicable way, he was sure it was there he would be able to find himself again. Or maybe for the first time.

Julian's move, however, had taken some adjustment. There were only limited museums and gourmet shops and department stores to provide distraction. And no shoulder-to-shoulder people on the streets among which to lose himself. He was not used to those microcosmic proportions. He was not used to so much solitude, so much time alone with only his thoughts. He was used to keeping in a crowd, on the move, out-maneuvering his own shadow. But day by day, the mountains worked their magic, and he began to find a certain solace and peace.

The clock on the night table glowed 12:47. Julian turned on the lamp. Next to it, in a matte black frame, he kept a photograph of him and Sam taken three years before. In it, their heads were slanted toward each other. They were laughing. They were happy. Julian picked up the photo, examined his own image. How could he still look so deceptively the same on the outside—tall, lean, slightly aquiline nose, stubborn locks of gold-brown hair falling onto his brow—when on the inside, grief and loneliness ached in every thirty-nine year old bone?

Julian caressed the glass with his fingertips. To the eye, it was merely a photograph, flat and motionless, a frozen slice of ordinary Sunday afternoon, a unique but unspectacular moment pressed in two dimensions. But looked at through the heart, it was round and warm and moving, an image Julian could fall into, a cloud of living memory floating him back to a time before death had dared to show its face. He pressed his lips to the vibrant, beautiful Sam who had once been. "I love you forever," he whispered.

Carefully setting the photo down, Julian slipped out of bed. Something distant yet familiar pulsed within him begging for attention. Maybe he was hungry. He felt his way along the dark hallway into the kitchen. Recessed overhead lighting lent a soft glow to the white refrigerator and range top and renovated oak cabinets with their white porcelain knobs. Julian leaned against the pantry door munching on a cluster of grapes. The French coffee press he'd recently bought winked silver from the slate blue countertop. He liked his new home, had enjoyed arranging furniture, hanging paintings, reading in the small enclosed porch off of its south side.

Julian was about to make a peanut butter sandwich, when a sense of creative urgency overtook him. Something larger than himself seemed to be directing him to the laundry room where he had stored a stack of unpacked boxes. A painting was straining for life. That's what it was. He hardly remembered what that felt like. Everything, he thought, had died with Sam, and not painting had become Julian's self-inflicted punishment for still drawing breath. The Muses gave up trying to cajole him out of endless mourning. Inspiration dried to dust. Now, despite himself, he was slipping through the season of endings and a spring of imagination was stirring again, welling from its center, luring him with its prism of possibility.

Numb to the chill of midnight or the fact he was barefooted and wore only briefs, Julian ripped the packing tape off several cartons marked "art materials" and fished in the crumpled newsprint with his hands. Locating what he was looking for, he lifted two boxes and followed the unfamiliar path to the easel propped in a corner of the spare bedroom. His last stretched canvas leaned beside it. From the carton filled with tubes of acrylic, he chose several and squeezed large ribbons of somber color onto a palette—umber, olive, crimson, ebony, ash. With broad strokes he began sweeping pigment across the canvas. He moved freely, wildly, as if this kind of urgent, uncensored inspiration had been lying dormant, waiting to resound when he had gotten quiet enough to hear it. But also as if some part of him knew where he was heading.

By the time Julian put down his brushes, the first light of day had pierced through a thin layer of cloud. He stepped back from his canvas to see what was birthing itself. Over transparent sweeps of color, a cathedral spire was taking shape. Crucifixes were evident in places. And slightly left of center, Julian saw the form of a man, a robed monk. How odd, he thought. He had never painted anything like that before. And he had never been so unaware of what translated itself onto his canvas. It was as if it had not even been his own hand that painted. For a while he contemplated the strange images before him, but soon realized he was very tired. "I'll figure *you* out later," he said to the monk, then headed down the hallway to his bedroom, crawled into bed, and fell instantly asleep.

CHAPTER 3

*It is no more surprising to be born twice than once.
Everything in nature is resurrection.*

—Voltaire

Lily stood at the door of Lovina's small white cottage. Flower boxes filled with petunias were anchored beneath the front windows. Below them, purple and pink azalea bushes, almost in full bloom, glistened in the mid-morning sun. Lily ran her fingers through her short, stylishly choppy hair as if to gain courage from the motion. She took a resolute breath. From a hook at the outside corner of the overhang, a wind chime made of tiny sea shells offered corroboration. She rang the bell. A large woman answered.

"Lily! I've been expecting you for a long time."

Lily glanced at her watch. It was just ten.

"Come in, dear. You're not late. Not at all."

What am I doing here? Lily thought. It was Maya, her young assistant at InWord Bound, who'd instigated this insanity. If it hadn't been for the dreams, Lily never would

have entertained the notion of seeing Maya's friend
Lovina, a psychic who heard the voices of spirits in an
M&M. But then the dreams had not seemed rational, so
Lily thought perhaps a degree of irrationality might be
needed to sort them out.

Lovina hummed as she led Lily through the living
room and into the dining room. A wave of purring, like a
feline chorus, broke out around her. "Egypt, India and
Peru," Lovina said, pointing to each of three cats.

Egypt was curled into an obsidian spiral at the inner
corner of the faded blue velvet sofa. India and Peru were
stretched out, nose to nose, along the window sill, tails
hanging in gray and white mirrored question marks.

"You could at least welcome our guest," Lovina said.

Egypt lifted her head and meowed.

"Yes. All right," Lovina replied. All three cats jumped
to the floor and lined up in single file behind her skirts
following like a gaggle of geese. Lovina directed Lily to a
dining room chair. "Would you like a glass of water?"

"No, thank you. I have my own." Lily lifted a bottle
of Evian out of her bag and placed it on the floor beside
her chair.

"I'll just get one for myself, then we can begin,"
Lovina said. She disappeared behind a white swinging
door.

Lily perused the room. Her gaze was drawn to the
prolific spider plants and trailing philodendrons that hung
from ceiling hooks in front of two double windows. Along
the only solid wall was a mahogany credenza on top of
which various begonias and African violets rested in trays
of pebbles. Lily had a love of gardening and noticed how

healthy and well cared for all the plants and flowers looked. But it was the cascading coral blooms of the Queen's Tears that, to Lily's mind, lifted Lovina into the realm of at least the horticulturally respectable. Queen's Tears did *not* flower for everyone.

Lovina returned and sat down opposite Lily. "So what is it you think you don't know?" she said, as the three cats arranged themselves in a line beside her chair. They became still as sculpture.

Lily had been distracted by the mysteriously obedient creatures and wasn't sure she'd heard the question correctly. "Excuse me?"

"How can I help you, dear?"

"What exactly is it that you do?"

"I suppose you could say I access the bigger picture."

"O…kay," Lily replied, taking in Lovina's substantial presence. She was tall, maybe five feet nine, big boned and fleshy and looked to be a youthful sixty with round cheeks the color of ripe peach. Her eyes, which were deep and wide set, were an unusual pale iridescent green. Her hair was light brown with a silver streak that marked a bright path into the knot of the chignon pinned at her nape. And suspended from a gold chain around her neck hung a dazzling blue jewel, which stood out against the silky russet of her blouse.

"I'll explain as we go along," Lovina said. She reached for the large bag of M&Ms that lay near the center of the mahogany table. Next to it was a white porcelain bowl with a scalloped edge. Lovina tore off the corner of the package and poured its contents into the dish. "I especially like that blue has been added," she said. "Delicious color.

So many possibilities."

Lily thought when Lovina was not divining wisdom, she probably consumed its conduit one sweet morsel at a time.

Closing her eyes, Lovina recited an invocation asking for the presence of those spirits who could offer the highest vision. "Just because you're dead, doesn't mean you're smart," she explained.

"I've never considered that." Lily shifted in her chair.

Lovina then asked Lily to hold in her mind the situation she wanted help with, and to place her hands just above the M&Ms. "In a minute," she said, "I'll scoop up a handful and let them fall into whatever pattern they choose for you." She turned on a small tape recorder. "Do you have any questions before we proceed?"

"Why M&Ms?" Lily had to ask.

Lovina smiled. "Ah, why not? The spirits do have a sense of humor. Let me tell you something about M&Ms. M&Ms are a lot like life. The outer shell can be thought of as the illusion, the thing that takes a shape, a form. The chocolate is what seems hidden inside. Some would call it Source or Mystery or God. Without the shell, what's at the center would dissolve and melt into everything as you tried to hold it. It would still have all its sweetness, but it could not be easily contained. And yet the center is what shaped the shell in the first place. Do you understand?"

"I think so," Lily replied, amused. There was something cheerful about the idea of God as chocolate.

"There is nothing without significance, my dear."

The woman loves her aphorisms, Lily thought.

Lovina reached toward the M&Ms.

"Would it be all right if I did that?" Lily said.

"If you'd like."

Lily lifted out a handful of rainbowed candy and let it fall onto the polished table top. She watched as M&Ms scattered, bounced and flipped finally coming to rest in her newly formed personal oracle.

"We're ready," Lovina announced. Egypt, India and Peru shifted in unison, forming an arc of fur around her. Lovina studied the configuration on the table.

Lily watched. "What do you look for?"

"I use M&Ms the way some people use tea leaves or rune stones. It doesn't matter to the spirits what manner of invitation is used to summon them, you know. In this case I look at the colors and the landing pattern. Whether they settle separately, or if some rest, domino-style, against each other. And whether the m's are revealed or concealed, or fork to the north, south, east or west."

"I see," Lily said, with transparent irony.

"I don't *need* M&Ms, my dear. I use them because most people feel more comfortable with some tangible and personal point of reference."

"Forgive me. This is all a little strange."

Lovina smiled, but didn't offer anything more in her own defense. "Shall we continue?"

"Yes, please."

Lovina again perused the constellation of bright dots. "Hmm. This is interesting. You have many m's forking to the east, which indicates illumination and clarity, and there's an abundance of yellow. You're a writer, yes?"

Lily nodded. She thought perhaps Maya had mentioned this to Lovina.

"Yellow shows up for many writers. For you, it indicates that writing, poetry especially, will help you at this time. While history is hardly ever truth, and fiction is only sometimes truth, poetry is always truth."

Finally something I can agree with, Lily mused.

"Now here, and almost at the very center, are two overlapping tidbits—one red and one blue. This signifies that your greatest illumination will come through a relationship, one in which each of you is seen as primary, like these two colors, totally whole unto the self. Yet, when the two of you merge, you will become something different, just as red and blue become violet. I will tell you, however, that on a scale of emotional intensity from one to ten, overlapping M&Ms indicate about a seventeen. This will be no ordinary love affair. This relationship will stir forgotten passions that rest at the center of everything that matters. Do you understand?"

"No, I'm afraid I don't exactly understand. Are you telling me there will be an intense relationship coming into my life?"

"Yes, that's what I see."

Lily didn't want to hear that the kind of passion she'd worked hard to avoid would come knocking at her door, even if she did secretly long for it. She debated whether or not to ask for more details, but opted for letting her life unfold without any further divination from Lovina. Especially since she didn't know how much of it she believed anyway. Was she supposed to take this bizarre woman seriously, prophesizing some kind of grandiose cosmic relationship from a handful of M&Ms?

"You may find my methods strange, my dear," Lovina

said, "but let me assure you I do not take my work lightly.

"You can read my *mind*?"

"I can *feel* your *thoughts*," Lovina replied. "In truth, there are no secrets."

Lily felt a sudden rush of air and wrapped her sweater more tightly around her. Her left palm began to itch the way it did whenever she lied to herself. During her last two years with Michael it had been a frequent annoyance. Only when Lily owned that her marriage had run its course, had dead-ended into a pit of apathetic resignation, did the itching cease. And here it was, back again. What am I trying to keep from myself now? she wondered. Her throat felt tight and dry. She reached for her water and took a sip. She fought the feeling that Lovina's predictions might be telling her it was time to come out of her emotional convent. That the dreams might be attempting to tell her the same thing. She scratched her palm.

"Now, my dear," Lovina said, "do you have specific concerns you'd like to discuss?"

"Yes. I guess so." Lily thought she might as well address what she'd come for. "Lately, I've been having this recurring dream of a young n..." she began.

Lovina interrupted. "Ahhh, the dreams! Yes!"

"You know about the dreams?"

"Of course," Lovina replied. "I do my homework. But I'm afraid I am not going to be able to shed much light on this. It's something which must and will be revealed to you in its own time. What I *can* tell you is that in these dreams you're trying to remember something from another time and place, something you have never completely resolved within your self."

"Are you talking about something from my childhood?"

"I'm talking about something from another lifetime, very long ago."

"Another lifetime?"

It was not that Lily hadn't pondered the idea of reincarnation. It was just that she'd never had cause to consider it in such a personal context.

"No big deal!" Lovina replied.

Maybe not to you. Lily's mind skimmed the thought the dreams might be connected with this intense relationship Lovina was predicting with such certainty, but she didn't allow herself to dive beneath its surface. The dreams had already caused too many sleepless nights. The last thing she wanted to think about was intense drama in her waking life as well. With her bookstore and her garden and her writing, there was already enough demanding her attention.

"You also have a gift for dream communication," Lovina continued. "Do you remember how real your dreams used to be when you were a child?"

"It's true. I used to have very vivid dreams."

"Well, you're again coming to a time for knowing your dreams."

"I don't mean to be rude," Lily said, "but who are you, and how do you do what you do?"

"Let's just say *my* gift, and my agreement with you, is to provide a light in the fog, so to speak. Hiring Maya and finding your way to me was no fluke. There *is* method to the seeming madness. Mr. Shakespeare knew from where his inspiration came."

Lovina appeared to slip into a state of deep concentration, sometimes closing her eyes as if to focus upon something behind them. "There is a kind of ordered spontaneity that runs through all things," she continued. "Choice is always available, and the growth is in experiencing the results of our choices, but all choices ultimately lead to the same place. And that's something for you to think upon until the next time we meet."

"The next time?" Lily wondered if she had a choice about that.

Lovina's face became a study in compassion. "We *will* meet again, my dear. And I'm afraid by then, even though you'll have found some of the answers you are looking for, you will have far more questions than you can now anticipate."

Lily found herself staring into the enigmatic, hypnotic face across the table. It was a face that caused her previous understandings to waver around the edges, even disappear in places leaving small gaps. Lily tried to will herself back to the old oak of her ideas, but already tiny, untried seedlings were anchoring themselves beneath the surface, waiting to push their new shoots into view.

Chapter 4

You Know, beloved, as the whole world knows how much I have lost in you, how at one wretched stroke of fortune that supreme act of flagrant treachery robbed me of my very self in robbing me of you; and how my sorrow for my loss is nothing compared with what I feel for the manner in which I lost you.

—Letter 1. Heloise to Abelard
The Letters of Abelard and Heloise

InWord Bound was busy. Customers were browsing the shelves or thumbing through back issues of Ploughshares and Glimmer Train, which lay on the table beside the cushy green sofa at the rear of the shop. Some were making purchases. Lily shifted between attending the register and sorting through the two stacks of second-hand acquisitions that crowded the ledge beneath the counter. Visible were a collection of dance photographs by Max Waldman, and A.S. Byatt's, Possession. Next to them, set safely aside, was a rare first edition of Edna St. Vincent Millay's sonnets, Fatal Interview.

Lily had owned her bookstore for almost three years. It was the fulfillment of a dream which, during the nine years she had been married to Michael, had never been realized. There were always time constraints and practical considerations and other financial priorities. Now, she was finally seeing her vision take on the substance of success. And she was doing what she enjoyed—selling and trading new, used and rare books, mostly arts and literature, to those, like herself, with a passion for words. On quiet days, when she had time to work on her poetry, Lily often called upon a ghostly Keats or Yeats or Dickinson for inspiration. She imagined that being in the mere presence of inspired language it would seep, as if by artistic osmosis, into her own writing.

Roomy yet intimate, InWord Bound was a place where people felt comfortable browsing, reading or even writing. In addition to the sofa, there were several quiet corners with soft lighting where customers could curl up in an arm chair or on a floor cushion and lose themselves in the timelessness of great art. In spring and summer, Lily kept a large vase filled with fresh cut flowers from her garden. Their fragrance wafted through the aisles of bookshelves on the currents of Vivaldi, Gershwin, Philip Glass, Carlos Nakai—whatever struck her fancy. In fall and winter, there was the aroma of hot apple cider or freshly brewed peppermint tea, which Lily offered her customers to warm a chilly afternoon.

Almost to the bottom of the stack she was working on, Lily reached for the next book—*The Letters of Abelard and Heloise.* Feeling a strange compulsion, she randomly opened it.

> Up to now I had thought I deserved much of you, seeing that I carried out everything for your sake and continue up to the present moment in complete obedience to you. It was not any sense of vocation which brought me as a young girl to accept the austerities of the cloister, but your bidding alone, and if I deserve no gratitude from you, you may judge for yourself how my labours are in vain. I can expect no reward from God, for it is certain that I have done nothing as yet for love of him. When you hurried towards God I followed you, indeed, I went first to take the veil—perhaps you were thinking how Lot's wife turned back when you made me put on the religious habit and take my vows before you gave yourself to God. Your lack of trust in me over this one thing, I confess, overwhelmed me with grief and shame. I would have had no hesitation, God knows, in following you or going ahead at your bidding to the flames of Hell. My heart was not in me but with you, and now, even more, if it is not with you it is nowhere; truly, without you it cannot exist. See that it fares well...

"Excuse me."

Lily did not notice the woman in front of her at the register.

"I'd like to buy this."

"I'm sorry," Lily said. She pulled herself into focus and closed the book. Something shapeless and uncomfortable inside of her began to shift around.

The woman handed Lily a copy of *Winter's Tale* by Mark Helprin. Lily rang up the sale. "Would you like a bag?"

"I'll just put it in mine," the woman replied.

Lily placed an InWord Bound bookmark in the paperback and handed it to her. "Thank you. I know you'll enjoy it. It's an extraordinary read."

When the store traffic thinned out, Lily, again, randomly opened *The Letters*.

In my case, the pleasures of lovers which we shared have been too sweet—they can never displease me, and can scarcely be banished from my thoughts. Wherever I turn they are always there before my eyes, bringing with them awakened longings and fantasies which will not even let me sleep. Even during the celebration of the Mass, when our prayers should be purer, lewd visions of those pleasures take such a hold upon my unhappy soul that my thoughts are on their wantonness instead of on prayers. I should be groaning over the sins I have committed, but I can only sigh for what I have lost. Everything we did and also the times and places are stamped on my heart along with your image, so that I live through it again with you. Even in sleep I know no respite. Sometimes my thoughts are betrayed in a movement of my body, or they break out in an unguarded word. In my utter wretchedness, that cry from a suffering soul could well be mine: 'Miserable creature that I am, who is there to rescue me out of the body doomed to this death?'...

The mysterious dream visions that haunted Lily

clicked open with the words she'd just read like keys in a series of mental locks. A spinning began in her solar plexus. She was staring into empty air when Maya, returning from an early dinner, approached her.

"Are you okay?" Maya said.

"Yes. I'm fine."

"You don't look fine."

"I read something that startled me for a minute. That's all."

"What was it?"

Lily knew Maya was no ordinary twenty-three year old. If anyone could understand what had set Lily spinning, it was Maya. While others her age were pre-occupied with their possessions and social lives, Maya was feeding a fascination for everything from Aboriginal mythology to Zen Buddhism, stretching her perceptions in every direction, coming to regard the phenomenal as ordinary. Lily had often seen miracles bloom like buttercups in the fields of her experience.

"Do you know who Heloise and Abelard are?" Lily asked.

"Sure."

Lily knew Maya didn't mean to sound flippant. It was just that she often stored the obscure information most people threw away.

"Peter Abelard was a teacher, philosopher and theologian in 12th century France," Maya said. "And Heloise was his lover, then his wife. He was cruelly castrated, and afterwards, he became a monk and she a nun. Theirs is one of the truly tragic love stories."

A monk. A nun. Castration. A tragic love. The images

played in Lily's mind connecting themselves, uncomfortably, to the visions and feelings she'd experienced in her dreams—the unapproachable monk with the frightened, prayerful eyes; the young nun, filled with inconsolable sadness and longing.

"I've been having some strange dreams these past weeks," Lily said.

"About what?

"A monk and a nun." Lily paused. "Did you know I went to see Lovina?"

"No! What did you think? She's cool, huh?"

"Awesome," Lily said, mimicking one of Maya's favorite expressions.

Maya laughed. "Did you ask Lovina about your dreams?"

"She said I was trying to remember something from another lifetime."

"Maybe you were Heloise."

"Right," Lily replied a little too sarcastically. Only Maya's mind could make such a sudden, unsubstantiated leap.

"It happens," Maya said. "No big deal."

"That's what Lovina said."

Maya swept her heavy, recently plum-tinged hair away from her face. "Are these books ready to be shelved?" she asked. She seemed to have no investment in Lily's possible past lives.

"Yes. Please." Lily watched Maya gather the stack and begin to walk away when the impulse seized her. She slid *The Letters of Abelard and Heloise* off the top of the pile. "Maya, what do you know about this reincarnation thing?"

"In many schools of thought, it's just what's so. People tend to glamorize and romanticize it too much."

"But we're not talking about some anonymous Egyptian temple dancer," Lily said. "These are historical figures, people you read about in books. It's egotistical and implausible to think you might have been someone like that. It's like people claiming they were Cleopatra or Beethoven or Michelangelo."

Maya smiled. "Everybody had to be somebody."

"Cute," Lily said, yet she often found Maya's equanimity refreshing. "I'm thinking of leaving a little early this evening. I know it's a late night, but would you mind closing? I'll make it up to you."

"No problem."

Lily completed some paperwork, then headed toward the small back room that housed files and coats and personal belongings. "Thanks," she said, when she returned. "There's only one more stack to be shelved. I'll be home shortly. Call if you need me."

Lily left and walked through the garage to her car. She got in and tossed *The Letters of Abelard and Heloise* on the seat next to her. She was tired. She didn't want to think about other lifetimes, M&M psychics, or an eight hundred year old correspondence that seemed disturbingly familiar. All she wanted was to go home and soak in a hot tub.

As she pulled onto the highway, a ribbon of late sun streamed through the window illuminating *The Letters* in an eerie golden light. Lily glanced at the glaring aura. It seemed to be widening, growing brighter, more brilliant. She thought of *Raiders of the Lost Ark*, when that awesome but terrible light was unleashed and Indiana Jones shouted,

"Don't look! Whatever you do, don't look!" With eyes steadfastly on the road, Lily reached over and shoved the book deep inside her bag.

When she finished dinner, Lily ran a bath and climbed in. The fragrance of lavender oil rose from the steamy water, infusing the air. She scooped liquid handfuls and streamed it down her arms and shoulders, smoothing the scent over her skin. She felt bony and fragile. She hadn't had her usual appetite in a while and she hoped she wasn't becoming too thin. Even though she was grateful she had the slender, if not toned, body of a dancer (she hadn't taken a ballet class in years), to Lily most dancers looked anorexic—unhealthy and unattractive. She didn't want to appear that way. Sliding more of herself into the soothing warmth, Lily closed her eyes, trying to quiet the cacophony of thoughts and images that once again rushed madly through her in dizzying configurations.

Maybe you were Heloise. Lily replayed Maya's words thinking how she had suggested this so casually, as if it were the most ordinary thing. But to Lily it was not ordinary. If she knew for certain not only that she had lived before, but when and where and who she had been, it would be most extra-ordinary. It would change everything. Or would it? she wondered. In this lifetime she'd still be Lily Sophia Richards. She'd still go to sleep and wake up in her own little corner of the universe. Maybe it wasn't so much the idea of reincarnation that disturbed her as it was the suggestion she might have been someone of Heloise's historic reputation. If that were proven true, she knew she would have to look at her dreams at least in a very different way, and that might change many things.

After her bath, Lily got into bed and curled up with the latest issue of *Poetry*. Poetry's always truth. At least Lovina had gotten that right. By ten o'clock she felt sleepy and turned off the light. I'd give anything for some good rest, she thought, as she arranged her pillow and pulled the covers around her. But the cosmos wasn't bargaining. At two in the morning Lily found herself wide awake, recording a different version of a familiar scenario. The dream had returned. With a new face. Literally.

In her journal, she wrote:

Most of the dream was the same, except now, the distant, despondent monk was overlaid with the animated face of a man, maybe in his late thirties, from this time. He had an exquisite smile and gorgeous blue blue eyes the same unreal color as the jewel I saw around Lovina's neck, eyes that seemed to cast a bridge of light from past to present. That's the only way I know to describe it. I was mesmerized by him. Seduced by his gaze. In the dream, I reached out to him in the same way the nun reached toward her monk. And the strangest part was that I felt as if I knew him. Not casually, but intimately and forever.

Lily put her pen down and closed her eyes. His face was still there. She tried breathing rhythmically for a couple of minutes, hoping to relax enough so she could fall back to sleep, but it didn't seem to be working. She opened her eyes and began to flip backwards through her journal scanning other dream entries she had made over the weeks, when something she'd completely forgotten leaped out at her. There it was, clear as day, the confirmation she needed. After one of the earlier dreams, Lily had awakened with an archaic, unlikely exclamation clearly embedded in her mind. Now she realized it was the same exact quote she had opened to in Heloise's letter, the words that had caused her solar plexus to spin—*Miserable creature that I am, who is there to rescue me out of the body doomed to this death*?

CHAPTER 5

*Some people will tell you dreams do not appear
to the naked eye, as ghosts do not appear or the
past cannot appear. They are sleeping too soundly
and forgetting themselves. Someone should shake
them. Someone should wake them up.*

—Julie Kate Howard

The sky had rumbled ominously, but opened only once in a brief downpour that left a shimmer of light on the wet, new leaves. Now the late afternoon sun slid through the window glass. It blinded Julian for a moment as he crossed the living room looking for his keys.

The Muses had descended upon him with the force of Zeus, himself, shifting his usual focus, often instigating the displacement of a wallet, a half-empty coffee mug...or a set of keys. Something creative and profound was happening, that much Julian knew, but he couldn't wrap his mind around it. Only his brush seemed able to translate the experience in any meaningful way. Color, movement, light—that was its language.

From the first unusual painting three weeks before, Julian found himself working in a way alien to him. Inspiration had always come more slowly, in measured segments. He had control over it. But now, time disappeared in front of a canvas as if he'd dissolved, trance-like, into it. And yet there was a feeling of effortlessness as his brush, almost of its own volition, dabbed and stroked and swirled itself into artistic life.

The subject matter, however, perplexed him—a cathedral, not unlike Notre Dame, in various stages of completion, a robed monk in ecstatic thought, or surrounded by books. Or a scene in which the monk's hands were positioned protectively over his groin, the look of terror in his eyes, an image Julian found deeply disturbing. He didn't know what to make of it. From some recess of his mind, the distressing thought of castration surfaced, along with a visceral wave of nausea.

Going through the house for the third time in search of his keys, Julian again checked his dresser. He looked once more in the pockets of the jacket he had worn earlier that day, and on the refrigerator door where they usually hung from a magnetic hook. He looked underneath the living room sofa, all around his studio, inside the basket on the kitchen counter where an odd assortment of orphaned items lay piled at its center. A city dweller for so many years, he had learned to take extra care when it came to his keys. Now he was annoyed by his apparent negligence.

Julian had finally accepted a dinner invitation from a couple he'd met through some New York friends. They'd been wanting to get together with him for weeks. He thought perhaps an evening out would do him good, help him put things into some kind of perspective. He would go downtown a little early, walk around a bit. But now he wondered if the Muses had other ideas, since his keys seemed no where to be found.

"Come on guys," he said. "Where are they?" Julian was not in the habit of talking to unseen company, but somebody must have been listening, because in the next minute, he found himself opening the front door, where he saw the keys still dangling from the lock. "Damn!" he said. He must have left them when he carried in the groceries that afternoon.

He remembered the only other time that had happened. It was over eight years before. His friend CJ had had a new show opening at a Soho gallery. Tired from painting all day, Julian had debated whether or not to go, yet a sense of something important cajoled him. He showered and dressed and was ready to leave when he couldn't find his keys. Just as he had now, he looked for them everywhere, only to discover they'd been left in the lock.

When Julian had arrived at the gallery, he was immediately drawn to a man standing alone, studying the painting before him. A couple of inches shy of Julian's six feet, the man had dark hair, which fell loosely around his head in soft curls. He wore a black jacket over blue jeans and a black silk shirt, and although Julian would later find he was five years older, he looked a perfect match to his own thirty-one.

Who are you? Julian formed the thought and launched it on a mental wave. Slowly, the man turned, a look of concentration on his face as if he thought he'd heard someone call him faintly or from a distance. He smiled and walked toward Julian. "Sam Keaton," he said. Julian noticed Sam's eyes were different colors—one blue, one hazel green. He wondered if he saw the world through a broader spectrum. Together they gazed at the painting in front of them. Like the moment, it, too, was surreal—a maze of black and white passages with a tiny gold key shining at its center. "The key is everything," Sam said, and for the first time in a long while, Julian felt the elaborate maze protecting his fragile heart unwind.

Julian now pressed his hand over the small gold key he always wore on a chain around his neck. Sam had given it to him the day they'd moved in together. He lifted it in his fingers, repositioned it so it hung inside his shirt, close to his heart. He wondered if losing his keys a few minutes ago "meant" anything. He wasn't sure there could be anyone after Sam.

Lily had another thirty minutes before closing the shop. It was quiet and she involved herself in re-working some lines of a poem. For the past couple of weeks, the nun and monk seemed to have faded into the ethers from which they came, and her dream life had become relatively uneventful. Feeling more rested, she began to receive new writing inspiration. Now deep in her search for the perfect metaphor, she only quickly glanced up as Julian entered and disappeared down an aisle of books.

"Let me know if I can help you find anything," she called out.

"I will," Julian said.

A few minutes later, he approached the register with a collection of Gustav Klimt prints.

Lily rang up the sale and handed him his change. Only then did she come face to face with the startling recognition. There was no mistaking the still blue eyes and exquisite mouth she had seen in her vision. Sweet air hovered around him, like jasmine but not jasmine. Like the scent of dreams. A small gasp escaped her, not small enough, however, for Julian to overlook.

"Are you all right?" he asked.

"Yes," Lily said, although she felt as if her molecules were spreading out and she was losing herself between them. "For a moment I thought I recognized you from…somewhere, but I'm probably mistaken," she lied. She would have known those eyes in any reality.

Julian flashed a smile that could spark a universe. "It sounded as if you thought I was someone you didn't particularly want to run into."

"No, that's hardly it."

Julian's presence became unsettling and Lily needed to look away. She reached for the water bottle she kept beneath the counter and took a sip.

To Julian, Lily seemed familiar, but wavering, as if he had to squint through a fine mesh of seasons to recall her. "I'm sure I would have remembered you," he said. "Is it possible we could have met in New York? I moved here two months ago. I'm Julian. Julian Prince."

Of course, Lily thought. "Lily Richards," she said. "Actually I used to live in the city, but it's been over ten years since I left, and I don't go back very often."

"Now you've got me curious." Julian wondered why he felt so uncomfortably attracted to this...woman.

Some involuntary part of Lily compelled her to take a chance. Normally, she didn't jump quickly into intimate conversation with a stranger. "You'll probably find what I'm about to say quite bizarre. Nothing lately has felt very sane."

"I know what you mean," Julian said.

"You do?"

"Yeah. I've had some bizarre experiences myself these last few weeks. Go ahead. Try me. Where do you think you know me from?"

Lily hesitated, then said, "From a dream."

Julian appeared unshaken. "Tell me more."

"I saw your face, clear enough to recognize you now." Lily paused. "And there's something else. Are you sure you want to hear this?"

"Sure," Julian replied, but already he was not.

"Your face was superimposed over the face of a man I've seen in my dreams often these past weeks, a monk from another time. I woke up somehow knowing you and the monk were the same person."

"A monk?" This was no longer a benign conversation.

"Does that mean anything to you?"

"It might," Julian said, but a rush of adrenaline was fogging his mind, and he was feeling an urgency to fly out the door. "Look, I'm having dinner with some friends, and I'm already late. Maybe I'll stop in again when I have more time."

Outwardly gregarious and charming, Julian was a deceivingly private man, now disturbed not only by what

Lily seemed to know about him, but also by how much he had not known about himself. He tried to sound neutral. "Well, good-bye," he said.

But his face recited something very different. For a moment, Julian's eyes drew Lily into a place beyond words, beyond time, beyond anything reasonable.

"Good-bye," Lily echoed, as Julian turned and walked briskly into the night.

On his way to the restaurant, Julian willed himself to put his encounter with Lily and everything it might mean out of his mind. He thought about the color of evening, how hungry he was, whether or not he would find his dinner companions personable, and by the time he reached La Bonne Auberge, he had succeeded.

Some deep part of Lily, on the other hand, wanted her to remember everything. All that remained, however, were fragments of conversation swirling in a cacophonous mental vortex. The few syllables that stood clearly apart were his name. *Julian.* She rolled it on her tongue, through her mind, recorded it in soundless spaces that rang to her soul. She steadied herself against the counter, attempting to draw from it some solidity. This was the feeling she'd tried so hard to protect against, but despite every effort, all her walls were crumbling.

CHAPTER 6

When Lily married Michael, she'd known in some deep place she hadn't felt all that was required. Strawberries did not taste sweeter, nor did colors appear richer. The air had not become more fragrant, and Michael's touch did not linger luxuriously on her skin like a wave of silk. It wasn't that she hadn't loved him—she had—but she came to realize they were, in essence, far apart. He was Rembrandt; she was Monet.

Like the buildings he designed, Michael needed reliability and longevity. Though he tried to accommodate Lily's spontaneous nature, Michael was infinitely more comfortable with routine. He always read for twenty minutes before falling asleep, hardly ever missed making his Sunday morning call to his parents. And Michael counted on a dinner salad to contain mainly lettuce, celery, plum tomatoes and cucumber. He did not handle the unexpected artichoke heart well.

Lily thrived on change. For her, rearranging the living room furniture or experimenting with a new, exotic recipe could satisfy an imaginative impulse, or completely transform a melancholy afternoon. And writing—whenever the unpredictable creative impulse overcame her—was as vital to her as breath. She expected Michael to understand. He expected her to remember the load of wet laundry that needed to be put into the dryer, and not to leave a sink full of dirty dishes overnight when it was her turn to wash them.

Despite their differences, Lily might have stayed with Michael even longer than nine years. Although a certain depth of connection had always been missing in their relationship, Michael was kind, generous and amusing at times, and Lily grew comfortable with him. But when she'd felt lured by something more expansive, something far beyond comfortable, she wondered if she'd perhaps sacrificed too much. Eventually, their marriage took an irreversible twist and broke apart.

Soon afterwards, Lily moved to a lovely house on two and a half acres, fifteen minutes from downtown Asheville. It was perfect, secluded yet not isolated, a contemporary cottage with lots of glass and light. Unlike Michael, an architect who had been partial to compact spaces and weighty woods that proved they could withstand the test of time, Lily had never liked living in older houses. Their confines had often felt uncomfortable to her. Too many dark, cramped corners. Too much charged history seeping from the painted and papered-over layers of the assorted lives that had been lived there. She felt more at ease in newer, lighter environments with a freer architecture.

Checking on some new bromeliads she'd placed in the bathroom greenhouse window, Lily caught her reflection in the mirror over the sink. She glided toward it, sure it radiated the newness she was feeling. She still moved with a familiar grace. Her hair was still short, her eyes gray-green flecked with gold. She eased her fingertips over the hollow of her cheeks, enjoying their natural smoothness. Even with its wide jaw and the fine lines that marked her well beyond innocence, Lily thought it a good face, now made luminous by the light from some inside sun. This was the feeling she had not experienced with Michael, the passion she had both feared and hoped for.

Lily went into the kitchen and removed a pint of chocolate ice cream from the freezer. She scooped out a spoonful and let the smoothness linger on her tongue. Ella Fitzgerald sighed sweetly from the stereo, singing as if she understood. *You go to my head, with a smile that makes my temperature rise, like a summer with a thousand July's, you intoxicate my soooul with your eyes...* Lily swayed her hips to the music's sensual rhythm. For a few enchanted minutes, she allowed herself to bask in possibility.

But once Lily remembered, the spell was broken. She remembered she had no idea whether or not Julian felt what she did or ever would, and a heaviness came crashing down on her. I must be mad, she thought, tossing the not-quite-empty container in the trash. I'm acting like a fool. And over a man I might never even see again.

Intent on distracting herself from this turn of mood, Lily flipped on the outside lights, filled a large watering can and carried it out to the patio. It was a little before sunset, but a growing blanket of clouds began to obscure the richest colors of the day. Not sure whether or not it would rain, Lily fed the thirsty geraniums she recently transplanted into round clay pots. She contemplated what to put in the planters on either side of the French doors.

Her flowers were the only thing besides poetry that could take Lily out of her own way. There was certainty in the yearly resurrection of fiery Fosterana tulips with their brilliant black and yellow eyes, and in the delicate magenta veins, like perpetual trails, on the white velvet of Japanese iris. She usually found it difficult to remain disheartened in such reassuring presence. But since encountering Julian, the only thing that seemed anywhere near certain was uncertainty. Even her own identity seemed questionable.

Lily felt a few drops of rain. She removed the cushions from the patio furniture and placed them inside the combination bench and storage bin she'd had specially built. The wind picked up a bit, then subsided. She grabbed the empty watering can and went into the house.

Afraid of what else she might discover, Lily hadn't touched *The Letters of Abelard and Heloise* since she'd brought the book home and stuck it on a crowded shelf. The little she'd read had been too real, too emotionally immediate. Now, in a defiant state, she convinced herself this was as good a time as any to learn what had gone on between them, what, in some way, might still be going on between them. Who was this tortured nun whose dreams have somehow become her own? Who was this ancient monk disguised in Julian's face?

Lily sat curled at the corner of the couch, the soft white light from a raku-based lamp illuminating the room. The rain tapped a syncopated rhythm on the rooftop— slow at first, then picking up speed until it settled into the soothing, even beat of a spring shower. Lily opened to the first letter, *Historia calamitatum*: Abelard to a Friend: The Story of His Misfortunes.

> There are times when example is better than precept for stirring or soothing human passions; and so I propose to follow up the words of consolation I gave you in person with the history of my own misfortunes, hoping thereby to give you comfort in absence. In comparison with my trials you will see that your own are nothing, or only slight, and will find them easier to bear...

Lily learned of Abelard's younger years in Brittany, of his education, and of his subsequent reputation as a brilliant teacher and philosopher. She read about the enemies who, threatened by his popularity and controversial theology, plotted to destroy him; and how, despite many obstacles, he arrived back in Paris where students flocked to attend his debates, and Heloise, without knowing it, awaited him.

Lily became absorbed in the story of a forbidden passion severed by the circumstances that birthed it. Through a twist of time, she felt Heloise perched at the hard edge of her bed inside the damp, dimly lit convent walls of The Paraclete reading those same words. The letter she had accidentally come across. The writings of the man who had once been her lover and husband. Heloise pressed the heavy sheaves to her heart, and, through tears as deep as her love, she—like Lily—drowned herself in the resurrected pieces of a former life.

It was well after midnight when Lily collapsed into a pain that hurt to the marrow of her. Conflicted feelings of anger, love and longing made it impossible to think of sleep. She felt the truth of what she'd read and grieved as if she, too, had lived it, as if the curtain of time between "then" and "now" had vanished. If this was about a "past" life, how could the past feel so present? Heloise was inside her, flooding her with ancient memories. Lily didn't know how to define what was happening. Whatever one might call it, she and Heloise had become the same tangle of sufferance, and Lily wanted her separate, familiar self back.

The seemingly senseless tragedy, which Lily could not free from her mind, was wrenching—the act of mutilation to Abelard which, for Heloise, was beyond all forgiveness; the religious suffocation of Heloise's vibrant, passionate youth; the separation from her son and from the man who was her own soul. Yet Heloise had held onto her love as the one beacon in the black circumstances of her days, the one light that shone greater for her than any God's. Lily wondered how much of Abelard Julian might carry within him, what tortured shapes might lie dormant behind that still beautiful countenance.

A cloudy, disquieting feeling washed over her. She bolted from the couch and headed into the study. She remembered something. Pulling out old notebooks and loose papers, Lily finally located what she was looking for—a certain journal and series of poems she'd written nearly three years before, shortly after she and Michael divorced.

At the time, Lily had no idea what her words meant. Images that did not seem to have any bearing upon her own experience spilled out of her mind and onto the page with an uncanny ease and familiarity. She had written in her journal —

I've been writing some very bizarre stuff lately. Poems about two lovers, vignettes from their lives written from the woman's perspective. They have an ancient feeling about them, and references to things I have no personal experience with—a convent, a child, a lover's "wound." Nothing quite like this has ever happened before with my poetry. Sure, I know what it feels like to write from an inspired space, but this is different. I can always, somehow, personally relate to what comes out on the page, but with these poems, it's as if this woman is telling her story through me, sort of using my mind and my hands to get it out. Maybe all this weirdness has something to do with separating from Michael. Maybe my mind finally has the freedom it needs to spread its junk all over the place—without having to clean it up!

Lily scanned several pages. She was astonished. *I've got to call Sara.* She looked at the clock. It was nearly two. She would have to wait until morning. Over-tired and overwhelmed, Lily undressed and climbed into bed. Her mind spun with the implications of what seemed to be happening. How could she, without knowing their history, have written about Heloise and Abelard all those years before? And from Heloise's intimate perspective? Heloise had been courageous, a thing Lily hoped she could find in herself, because, without knowing exactly why, she had the certain feeling she would need it.

CHAPTER 7

The past is still, for us, a place that is not safely settled.

—Michael Ondaatje

"Astralabe?" Sara said, eyebrows raised. "Heloise named her son Astralabe?" Sara had joined Lily for breakfast at The Sunrise Café.

"It's bizarre, isn't it," Lily said. "It's actually the name of a medieval instrument used to determine the altitude of celestial bodies."

Lily had waited weeks before she'd told Sara, her dearest friend, about the dreams, and about her reading with Lovina. She wasn't sure exactly why she'd hesitated, other than to give herself time to ignore or rationalize or will the visions away, none of which she'd been able to do. She also felt afraid even her best friend might think her on the thin edge of sanity. But as they'd talked, Sara proved to be reassuring.

"Something similar happened to me once," Sara had said. "Not quite the same, but an experience where places and things felt oddly familiar."

"Like what?"

"Like the time I was in Scotland on the Isle of Skye." Sara's eyes drifted off in the direction of memory. "Everything seemed oddly familiar and dear—the emerald hills, the purple moors. I remember feeling I'd somehow come home. It moved me to tears. It was one of those things you know is true, but you don't know how you know."

"Like what happens in my dreams," Lily said.

Now, over breakfast, Lily told Sara the heart-wrenching story of Heloise and Abelard—their passionate, forbidden love affair; how they were discovered by Heloise's uncle, who in his shame and rage, had Abelard castrated; how, afterwards, according to Abelard's wishes, they both took religious vows, thereby ending for Heloise any hope of a life together.

"The story is amazing." Sara took a slow sip of coffee. "Just like your dreams. It's the kind of stuff that would only be believable if you wrote it as fiction. Maybe you were Heloise in another life."

"That's what Maya suggested. She said everybody had to be somebody."

Sara laughed. She tucked silky strands of light brown hair behind her ears, broke off a large chunk of blueberry muffin and popped it in her mouth. "I suppose that's true in a reincarnational sense."

"It's more than that. Sometimes I can feel Heloise inside me as if she's still very much alive, as if she's both separate from me as Lily, yet part of who I am at a deeper place where there is no separation. And I think she's been there for a long time."

"What do you mean?"

Lily picked at her mushroom omelet with the tip of her fork. "Last night, I dug out some poems I wrote almost three years ago—a strange series with a voice that wasn't mine, and the kind of religious references I wouldn't have used."

"And they were about Heloise?"

"And Abelard. When I re-read them, I felt like I was in some kind of time warp."

"Did you bring them with you?" A freelance editor and writer herself, Sara shared Lily's love of words.

"Just a couple."

"Let's see."

Lily handed the poems to Sara. Not having much of an appetite, she only nibbled on the rest of her breakfast while Sara perused the pages. She was anxious about what her friend might think.

> What wretched misery
> To be the cause of your disgrace!
> What savage wound inflicted
> On your dearest flesh for my offense
> Of love!
> I've all but died from endless
> Shafts of Fortune's angry hand aimed
> At my heart —
> Our son, then you,
> Torn from my youthful breast.
> I cannot rest, but only suffer
> Long contrition

> Which will never make amends.
> No repentance
> Washes sins when old desire retains
> Its will.
> This convent, built by you, remains
> My prison still. Always
> Rather you than God I've tried to please.
> Now, as these impious bones bear
> Long and silent grief,
> I contemplate our former love, and sigh
> At how you've offered no relief.

"This doesn't sound anything like your poetry."

"I know." Lily eyed Sara with apprehension. "So what do you think?"

"I've only finished the first one, but it seems to be right out of their story."

"Read the other one, then I'll show you something else." Lily pulled *The Letters* from her bag.

"Why don't you finish eating."

"I think I'm done," Lily said. Food didn't appeal to her. Resurrecting those poems had kept Lily's stomach churning with anxiety all night and into the morning. She was not entirely comfortable showing them even to Sara.

"Give me a minute then."

Sara continued to read.

> In sin we were untouched
> by Heaven's hand,
> A warming fire before us
> as within our souls;

But then, united, Providence
required a stand,
And charged our pure devotion
with a Hellish toll.

What prompted me to marry you
and cause your fall —
Cornelia knew the truth
of this profound lament;
And if my cloistered life
is Fate's judicious call,
A reverential pose
proves not that I repent.

"What in the world did you make of these when you wrote them?" Sara said.

"I was terrified. Even though I was moved by the feelings expressed, I didn't have a clue as to what they meant. And the words came so quickly, I could hardly write fast enough. At one point, I was so freaked, I almost hurled them into the fire. But something stopped me."

"I can only imagine how frightening it must have been." Sara gave Lily a moment to sip her tea. "So do we know who Cornelia is?"

"She's from something called, *Pharsalia*, written by an ancient Roman poet named Lucan." Lily smiled at the absurdity of her situation. "It was in a footnote. Heloise was obviously familiar with her. Listen to this." Lily opened *The Letters* and located the first passage she had marked. "In the *Historia calamitatum*, Abelard writes—

'…There were many people, I remember, who in pity for her youth tried to dissuade her from submitting to the yoke of monastic rule as a penance too hard to bear, but all in vain; she broke out as best she could through her tears and sobs into Cornelia's famous lament:

> O noble husband,
> Too great for me to wed, was it my fate
> To bend that lofty head? What prompted me
> To marry you and bring about your fall?
> Now claim your due, and see me gladly pay.'"

"Whoa!" Sara took the last bite of muffin. "The odds of this kind of coincidence are pretty slim, I think."

Lily reached across the table with a napkin. "Hold still, you've got blueberry mouth."

Sara smiled. "Thanks, mom."

"It's very eerie. I've never heard of Cornelia, or her lament. I'll read you what I found in two of the four personal letters, okay?"

"I thought there were eight."

"There are, if you include Abelard's *Historia calamitatum*, but there are only four that deal with their past intimacies. The others involve religious direction."

"Let me get more coffee before you continue." Sara signaled to the waitress.

"How you can drink so much of that stuff and stay calm still mystifies me."

"I thrive on it. Especially since, with the help of a good friend, I gave up cigarettes." The waitress refilled Sara's cup for the third time. "So what else have you found?"

"I haven't read the letters closely, just skimmed through Heloise's looking for anything that might shed some light on the poems. There are several passages. This is from Letter 1. Heloise to Abelard—

'…Tell me one thing, if you can. Why, after our entry into religion, which was your decision alone, have I been so neglected and forgotten by you. Tell me, I say, if you can—or I will tell you what I think and indeed the world suspects. It was desire, not affection which bound you to me, the flame of lust rather than love. So when the end came to what you desired, any show of feeling you used to make went with it. This is not merely my own opinion, beloved, it is everyone's. There's nothing personal or private about it; it is the general view which is widely held… I wish I could think of some explanation which would excuse you and somehow cover up the way you hold me cheap…' "

Sara, motionless, seemed deep in contemplation.

Lily continued. "And from Letter 3. Heloise to Abelard—

'…O god—if I dare say it—cruel to me in everything! O merciless mercy! O Fortune who is only ill-fortune, who has already spent on me so many of the shafts she uses in her battle against mankind that she has none left with which to vent her anger on others. She has emptied a full quiver on me…

'…Moreover…while we enjoyed the pleasures of

an uneasy love and abandoned ourselves to fornication (if I may use an ugly but expressive word) we were spared God's severity. But when we amended our unlawful conduct by what was lawful, and atoned for the shame of fornication by an honourable marriage, then the Lord in his anger laid his hand heavily upon us, and would not permit a chaste union though he had long tolerated one which was unchaste...'"

"And you'd never seen these letters before you wrote the poems?" Sara said.

"Never." Lily searched for another page she'd marked. "I didn't even know they existed until the book found its way into my hands a few weeks ago at the shop. This is more from Letter 3. Heloise to Abelard—

'...What misery for me—born as I was to be the cause of such a crime! ...Is it the general lot of women to bring total ruin on great men? For this offense, above all, may I have strength to do proper penance, so that at least by long contrition I can make some amends for your pain from the wound inflicted on you...and thus make reparation to you at least, if not to God.

'For if I truthfully admit to the weakness of my unhappy soul, I can find no penitence whereby to appease God, whom I always accuse of the greatest cruelty in regard to this outrage. How can it be called repentance for sins...if the mind still retains the will to sin and is on fire with its old desires?

'...At every stage of my life up to now, as God knows, I have feared to offend you rather than God, and tried to please you more than him. It was your command, not love of God which made me take the veil. Look at the unhappy life I lead, pitiable beyond any other, if in this world I must endure so much in vain, with no hope of future reward…'"

Lily began to weep. "I can't read any more. It wrecks my heart."

Sara reached across the table and took her friend's hand. "It's understandable, Lil. This is not exactly your everyday occurrence."

"I guess it's affecting me more than I realized. And it may not be over yet." Tears trickled from Lily's tired eyes. "There's something I haven't had a chance to tell you."

"What is it?"

"The man I told you I saw in my dream, the one whom the monk turned into, showed up at the shop last week."

"You've got to be kidding." Sara straightened her back, leaned stiffly against the bench.

For a moment, it looked to Lily as if her friend was pulling away, and she wondered if she'd made a mistake taking Sara into her confidence. But in the next, she was sure she was overreacting, projecting onto Sara the judgment and doubt she'd already aimed at herself. "I'm not kidding," she said.

"Are you sure it was him?"

"There wasn't a second of doubt. On an impulse, I wound up telling him about my dreams, and when I mentioned the monk, he turned pale, made a polite excuse and left."

"Do you think he was also having dreams?"

"I don't know. All I know is I literally felt unsolid in my own skin, as if I were flying out of myself and toward him, trying to find a safe, warm place to land. I've never experienced anything like it. Part of me wished he'd never come into the shop, yet another part couldn't bear him walking out the door. Now I have no idea if I'll ever see him again."

"Did you find out his name?"

"Julian *Prince*. Can you believe it?"

"I guess at this point I can believe anything."

Lily became serious. "Do you think I could be losing it, Sara? The truth."

"No. I truly don't think you're losing it, but I do think something extraordinary is happening here. Look on the bright side, you probably have enough material to keep you writing for lifetimes."

"Very funny," Lily replied, but her vulnerable state again overtook her. "I need to be able to talk to you about this. You won't think it's all too bizarre and abandon me, will you?"

Sara squeezed the hand she was still holding. "Not a chance," she said.

CHAPTER 8

The truth is rarely pure and never simple.

—Oscar Wilde

Julian wanted to pretend nothing significant had happened between him and Lily. Denial could be convenient, but he knew trying to fool himself was a dangerous stance. He wished Sam were there to help him, to listen to him, to advise him. But really, what could Julian have said? I'm painting disturbed monks? A woman recognized me from a dream? I'm pulled toward this woman in a way I can't explain or comprehend? Although Sam had had the capacity to understand the spheres of the heart in a larger way than most, Julian didn't know how he could ever have explained Lily to him.

At times, Julian felt as if he were on the verge of some exhilarating yet terrifying discovery. Uncomfortable as it might be, he knew he was going to have to confront Lily, to find out why he was in her dreams and what she knew about a certain monk. He was going to have to look straight into her and face whatever might be reflected back.

It was a fine afternoon for apprehending truth. Rosy dogwoods laced a cerulean sky, bright cardinals lit scarlet against a curtain of emerald, and everywhere, daffodils and jonquils exploded in a hundred shades of sun. Life spun in every nook, and Julian was part of that life, part of the newness that burst, from some wondrous source, into bloom.

Julian entered InWord Bound. He saw Lily at the rear of the shop. On jelly legs he made his way down the aisle of bookshelves, toward where she was fluffing cushions.

"Lily?"

She turned sharply at the music of Julian singing her name.

"I don't know if you remember me..."

"Yes, of course I remember you," Lily replied. "Julian, right?" As if she could ever forget.

"Do you have time to talk, maybe get a cup of coffee?"

"Sure. All right. I'll just let my assistant know I'm going out." Despite a feeling of inner disintegration, Lily tried to appear in control of herself. She went in search of Maya as Julian headed for the door. She met him there. "There's a café a few doors down the street," she said.

"Sounds fine."

Lily and Julian walked the half-block in silence. They found the café relatively empty for a mid-afternoon. Lily's was a familiar face at Martinique's, and she and Julian were greeted by Amy, the hostess. They were escorted to a quiet table near the back.

Lily struggled to keep her eyes from invading every

inch of Julian—the jagged lengths of hair that fell over his brow, the crease in his right cheek when he smiled, that place between his collarbones his opened shirt buttons revealed.

Within a few minutes, their superfluous tea and coffee before them, Julian began to form his feelings into words.

"I'm sorry if I seemed to leave abruptly the other evening. I didn't know how to respond to what you were telling me. About your dreams. I was a little shaken."

"Are you saying what I said made sense to you?"

"Nothing these days makes actual sense to me, but, yes. I'm a painter, and since moving to Asheville, my work—really my whole life—has taken a turn I haven't been able to understand. Inspiration hits me—that's just how it feels—it hits me with such intensity that I'm unable to resist it, even at three in the morning. And I don't always know where I'm going as I paint. But the most astonishing thing is what's been appearing on my canvases. Crucifixes. A cathedral spire I recognize as Notre Dame. And most bizarre, a monk who appears in many postures, one with terror on his face and his hands between his legs, which I somehow feel is because he's been, of all things, castrated. I began to wonder if your dreams and my paintings might be connected."

Lily stared incredulously at Julian. She was paralyzed by what he was saying.

Julian mistook her silence for judgment. "Maybe this wasn't such a good idea." He quickly got up and started to reach for his wallet. "I don't even know why I'm here. It's very unlike me."

"Please stay. I'm staring only because I'm amazed by what you just described. Maybe even a little terrified."

Julian cautiously settled back down.

"I'd like to see the paintings sometime."

"I don't think I'm ready to show them to anyone just yet. I can hardly look at them myself."

"Of course. I understand." Lily took a long sip of tea, fumbled with her napkin. "Can I ask you something?"

"I guess so."

"Do you believe in having lived other lives?"

"Why do you ask?"

"Answer me first, then I'll tell you why."

"I don't know what I believe at this point. The more bizarre my experiences become, the more I'm forced to consider that anything might be possible. It's gotten to where most of the time I think I'm just going to have to become very comfortable living with mystery."

"I know!" Lily recalled thinking those same words.

"So, why do you ask about other lives?"

"Julian," Lily loved the sound of his name, "I've never had a conversation quite like this before."

"Me neither, and right now part of me wants to bolt for the exit." Julian tenderly perused Lily's face, then lowered his gaze. "There's so much you don't know about me," he whispered.

Sensing Julian's reticence, Lily did not push for more. "I'm sure," she replied. "But we can leave those tales for another time."

Julian realized he'd been holding his breath. He released it. "So, do you think we've known each other before? Is that why you're asking me this?"

"I'll tell you a story and let you draw your own conclusions."

"Sounds fair."

"Shortly before the day you first came into the shop, I impulsively opened a book that came in, a book of letters. I discovered, from what was described, that I seemed to be dreaming the dreams of someone who had lived eight hundred years ago. Do you know who Heloise and Abelard were?"

"Didn't they have some kind of tragic history?"

"Do you want to know details?"

"Okay," he said. But the mention of Heloise and Abelard triggered an uneasy feeling in Julian. He suddenly remembered something that had happened a few months before, when he'd brought Sam's ashes to Paris, and he began to suspect there might be more going on here than he wanted to investigate. He pulled his attention back to Lily.

Lily relayed to him everything she had read. Julian stared at her transfixed or in shock, she wasn't sure which. "...And Julian, you might want to know that when Abelard taught at Notre Dame, it was still under construction."

Julian spun with layers of feelings he didn't imagine he owned. How could an eight hundred year old story gnaw at his center with the sharpness of contemporary teeth? Was the scholarly, prayerful, terrified monk in his paintings Abelard? "I don't think I can take in anymore right now," he said.

"I understand." A few moments of silence slipped between them before Lily continued. "When you left the shop the other evening, I didn't know if I'd ever see you again. Thank you for coming back and finding me." Lily's words spanned dimensions.

Julian smiled. "I felt I had to." For a moment, he reverted to his engaging self. "When a complete stranger tells me she recognizes me from a dream, and knows about a certain monk, well…how could I leave something that provocative alone?"

"Do you have regrets about pursuing it?"

"No. At least I don't think so. Not right now. I'm just feeling overwhelmed, like I need time to sort this through."

Lily took out her wallet.

"Please. This one's on me." Julian placed a five dollar bill over the check. "I think I'd better be going."

Lily knew she was about to tread on potential disaster. "Will I see you again?" She couldn't let this man walk out of her life for good.

The old Julian would have had no problem answering. Once he recognized that feelings were being directed toward him in a way he couldn't return, there would have been no ambiguity about his reply. But this new Julian felt things differently. His emotional boundaries were not so clear, and feelings seeped over them forming a puddle of confusion. Without understanding why, he found he could not tell Lily he was gay. "I don't know, Lily. Right now I have a lot to contemplate. Are you okay with that?"

"Yes. I'm fine," Lily said, even though she wasn't. She wanted to ask him for his phone number and address, but thought it might appear too pushy. "You know how to get in touch with me."

"Yes." Julian smiled, then turned and walked away.

Lily watched him through the window, his graceful presence diminishing into distant shadow. The rational part, the mind of her, argued that she was not going to dissolve herself into this man about whom she knew virtually nothing. She was not going to fall in love with some fantastic vision of him that might never become flesh.

The feeling part, however, the heart of her knew the truth. Her heart knew it was far too late, that she had become too insubstantial to hold the solid stance of reason, that she had given the largest part of herself to Julian a long time ago and he had owned it for centuries.

CHAPTER 9

I love somebody dearly,
I love somebody well.
I love somebody with all my heart,
'Tis more than tongue can tell.

Somebody's heart is faithful,
Somebody's heart is true.
Somebody waits for somebody,
Somebody knows, do you?

—North Carolina Folk Ballad

It had been two weeks since Lily last saw Julian, yet everywhere she turned, the air seemed filled with his jasmine. It clung to her like a second skin. In her weakest moment, Lily began to dial his number, which she'd looked up and kept filed under "emergency." She wanted to lose herself in the sound of him, to tell him his presence was all around her. But in some deep way, she knew she couldn't be the one to reach out. She could not quest after

Julian, but must instead wait for him to make the next move. He would have to seek her out again, and express the feelings she'd sensed he had for her. She was not going to make herself look the fool.

It was almost ten a.m. and Lily was still in bed. She didn't remember the last time she'd felt so lethargic. Completely unlike herself, she'd called Maya earlier and told her she had some personal things to take care of and would be out most of the day. How could she be so affected by Julian? It frightened her. In a practical sense, she hardly knew him. But the deeper connection she felt seemed far beyond practicality.

Lily stared at the ceiling for a long while, then perused the room. Unhung clothes were carelessly draped across the chair, the dresser top cluttered with make-up and used tissue, the rug unvacuumed. She could handle the occasional disarray in her house. It was inner emotional disorder Lily tried most to avoid. When it came to her heart, she wanted everything neatly in its unobtrusive place.

Forcing herself out of bed, Lily ambled toward the bathroom. There was nothing to do now but go about her life as best she could, to wait and see if Julian would contact her. When she'd washed and dressed and fixed a cup a tea, Sara called.

"What are you doing home? I called the shop and Maya said you wouldn't be in until late afternoon. Are you all right?"

"Relatively. I just didn't feel like facing the world today. I'll be fine."

"I have to go to Black Mountain to do some research

for my infamous novel. Why don't you come with me?"

At first Lily declined, but then decided she could use the change of scenery and Sara's companionship. She hoped her friend wouldn't mind listening to a few more things she'd read.

"Are you up to hearing a little more about Heloise and Abelard?"

"Absolutely."

Strolling through Black Mountain, trying to occupy herself with something other than her omnipresent phantom love, Lily accompanied Sara as she browsed old businesses and talked to people who remembered the Spanish Castle, and when Black Mountain had been called Grey Eagle. At least, Lily thought, the things these people recalled stayed within the boundaries of a lifetime. They didn't cruise through centuries, showing up on their mental doorstep in some clever but transparent disguise.

In the library, Lily helped Sara copy old folk songs and ballads —

> Oh, bring me back my blue-eyed boy,
> Oh, bring my true love back to me.
> Oh, bring me back my blue-eyed boy,
> And forever happy I will be.

"The librarian says there's an apple orchard on the other side of the mountain, about six miles," Sara said. She needed to scope it out since deciding that her characters, Cheryl and Gil, would have their first romantic encounter in an orchard. "Are you in a hurry to get back?" she asked Lily.

"No. Actually, I welcome the distraction."

Lily and Sara drove along the six winding mountain miles. It was a narrow passage with lush, towering peaks. As they came to the other side, the pavement began to level out. There was not much there, and no signs of any orchard. Sara decided to ask for directions and turned into the next driveway. She stopped about thirty feet in, just short of a very old, precarious-looking wooden slat bridge.

"This is as far as I'm going with the car," Sara said. "That bridge looks pretty shaky. I'll walk to the house. Do you want to come?"

"No, I think I'll wait here."

"I'll be back in a minute."

Lily pulled off her socks and tossed them on the floor mat next to her already discarded Reeboks. It was a warm spring day, and she enjoyed the freedom of bare feet. She slipped the soundtrack from the film, *Somewhere In Time* into the tape deck. Reclining her seat, Lily stretched her legs up against the dashboard and closed her eyes. Within seconds, Julian's face seemed to peer through the open window, a halo of sun framing his hair. Caught up in the vision, Lily moved her hand to touch his cheek. She swore she could feel the warmth of his breath on her fingers and the slight bristle of a day old beard.

Suddenly, the music swelled and deep strings reverberated through the stereo speakers signaling foreboding. Pulled back to the moment, Lily opened her eyes. The vision vanished. Somewhere in time...she thought, but didn't have a chance to follow any further.

Sara ran toward the car excited to tell Lily she'd serendipitously come upon Clarence Johnson, the manager of Todd's Apple Orchard. She scrambled for pad and pen and recorded what she'd learned in Apple Orchard 101. "I've got directions and permission to look around," Sara said, as they backed out of the driveway.

About half a mile down the road, they found the unpaved entrance and drove a short distance in. They decided to walk the rest of the way. At first, they took the wrong path. It was worth it. To the left, on a steep hill covered in vegetation, dozens of honeycombs peaked through thickly-laminated camouflage. Wild daisies and dandelions caressed their calves. To the right, the landscape opened onto rolling hills and corn fields bordered in the distance by the misty Swannanoa Mountains.

Lily remembered a game she'd played as a child. She picked a dandelion and made a wish. If she could blow all the seeds away with one breath, her wish would take root. She closed her eyes and whispered, "Julian." Three breaths later, her hopes were scattered on the wind.

"Let's rest for a minute," Lily said. The walk had been all uphill.

"Good idea."

They found a shady patch of green.

"So, what's going on?" Sara said.

"Nothing. That's the problem. I haven't heard from Julian since I told him about Heloise and Abelard."

"Why don't you contact him?"

"I can't. I feel too vulnerable expressing my feelings to him without wanting them to be returned. It would blow me away like dandelion fluff if they weren't. Also, for some reason, I feel I'm not supposed to go to him. I think part of this has to do with Heloise."

"Lily, do you suppose it really is a past life thing?"

"I don't know. Call it what you will, Heloise is here, inside me. I'm dreaming her dreams. And Julian is painting castrated monks. Whatever it is, I don't resist it anymore. And I can't figure it out. I've tried both and I'm exhausted."

"The dreams have come back?"

"On and off."

"I still think there's something inspiring hiding in these ashes."

"If you can be inspired by insanity," Lily said dryly.

"*Much madness is divinest sense to a discerning eye...* Sara recited. "At least according to our friend Emily." Sara smiled.

They shared a love of Dickinson.

"I guess that's one perspective." Lily twirled several tall blades of grass around her fingers. "Oh no!" Suddenly, Lily remembered she'd forgotten to water the flowers on the patio. And it wasn't the first time. Nor the second. She'd already lost a favorite white begonia to her absentminded emotional state.

"What is it?"

"My flowers." Lily's eyes filled with tears.

"What about them."

"I'm murdering them, Sara." Lily was into her drama. "I've been so spacey, I forgot to water them. Again."

Sara stroked Lily's arm. "They'll be all right, Lil."

Lily pulled away. "No. They *won't*."

Sara grew silent, as if she knew Lily was talking about more than her flowers and she didn't know what she could say to reassure her.

"I'm sorry, Sara." Lily was embarrassed by her outburst. "Forgive me."

"It's okay. It'll be okay." Sara picked a daisy and handed it to Lily.

Lily felt her defenses melt. "What would I do without you?" she said. For a few minutes they each sat in private contemplation.

Sara broke the silence. "So what else have you discovered about Heloise and Abelard? I'm fascinated by the whole thing, you know."

Lily put thoughts of her flowers aside. There was nothing she could do until she got home. "I've been obsessed with the letters. I've read them, the four personal ones, over and over, and they still move me to tears. And to anger. I've been beating a lot of pillows lately."

"Are you sure this is about Heloise and Abelard? Or is there some Lily and Julian in there?"

"I'm sure it's a little of both. But after reading how Abelard pretty much abandoned Heloise, I would say he deserves his share."

"Does he offer any explanation?"

"A poor one, as far as I'm concerned." Lily took *The Letters of Abelard and Heloise* out of a canvas tote bag with a Greenpeace logo. "I don't seem to go very far these day without this book." She continued digging and came up with a couple of apples. "Do you want one?"

Sara raised her eyebrows, seemingly amused by the irony of bringing apples to an orchard. "Thanks." She took a shiny Macintosh. "I guess we'll have to come back in a few months to get ripe fruit off these trees."

Lily smiled. She opened to the first page she'd marked. "Heloise first writes to Abelard after she comes across his *Historia calamitatum*. If you remember, she tells him how miserable she's been, and wants to know why, after their entry into religion, he's neglected her in her grief. I'm using some of their language as I paraphrase, okay?"

"It's fine. It helps me get a feel for them."

"When Abelard writes back, he basically ignores her personal distress, and goes on to detail the dangers and threats from his enemies that create daily fear in his life. He rambles for pages on the power of prayer and asks that Heloise and her nuns pray for him. And he asks, if he should die, that his body be brought to Heloise at The Paraclete for burial. As to why he neglected her for twelve years, he writes—

> 'If since our conversion from the world to God I have not yet written you any word of comfort or advice, it must not be attributed to indifference on my part but to your own good sense, in which I have always had such confidence that I did not think anything was needed; …If, on the other hand, in your humility you think differently, and feel that you have need of my instruction and writings in matters pertaining to God, write to me what you want, so that I may answer as God permits me…'"

Lily paused. "Can you believe that after all they were

to each other, this is the only thing he can address?"

"It's pretty pathetic, but it was a different time, Lily, with different rules."

"It still seems so cruel."

"Maybe under the circumstances Abelard felt it best not to encourage memories that could only bring about more pain."

"Maybe," Lily echoed, but she thought Sara too generous in her suggested explanation for Abelard's insensitivity.

Lily resumed the story. "Anyway, Heloise writes back and pours her heart out to him, confiding how tormented she's been, and how thoughts of their love-making, which she can hardly put out of her mind, never displease her. She urges him not to talk of death, for if she loses him, their would be nothing left to hope for, no reason to live. And she tells Abelard to stop praising her, that she's not strong, and that she needs his support."

"She's a lot more open than I would have expected a woman, and especially a nun, to be in the 12th century," Sara said.

"At the time of these letters, she must have been about thirty and Abelard fifty. She was the abbess of The Paraclete, the monastery Abelard originally founded."

"So how does Abelard respond?"

"Judge for yourself." Lily flipped to another page. "He writes back urging her to give up her 'old perpetual complaint against God.' He argues that his castration was an act of divine mercy and totally justified, and that if she really wants to please him in all things, as she claims, she must rid herself of her bitterness. He says God's punishment was more properly directed against them when they were married. He reminds her of the time she stayed at Argenteuil and he came to see her, and they made love in a corner of the refectory; of how he irreverently disguised her as a nun when she was pregnant; of how he forced her to make love during Lent when it was forbidden.

"Abelard sees their former passions not as acts of love, but as acts of lust and obscenity, and feels he was justly punished. He tells her God is mindful of her as well, since He planned for her conversion. He writes—listen to this, Sara!—

> 'What a hateful loss and grievous misfortune if you had abandoned yourself to the defilement of carnal pleasures only to bear in suffering a few children for the world, when now you are delivered in exultation of numerous progeny for heaven!'"

"Jesus! Lily."

"I know." Lily turned to the last page she had marked. "This is the final piece," she said, suddenly feeling a familiar but still unsettling melancholy spread through her that was not entirely her own. "Sara...thank you for bearing with me these months. You're the only one I've dared to tell about my dreams and how real Heloise's feelings are to me."

"You can tell me anything, Lil. You know that."

Lily rested for a moment in the reassurance of Sara's friendship, then lowered her gaze to the open pages in her lap. "So Heloise, obviously crushed but resolved to accept the fact that she has no emotional ally in Abelard, writes back only to ask for religious instruction. She begins, however, with this—her last words on the subject of her feelings.

'I would not want to give you cause for finding me disobedient in anything, so I have set the bridle of your injunction on the words which issue from my unbounded grief; thus in writing at least I may moderate what it is difficult or rather impossible to forestall in speech. For nothing is less under our control than the heart—having no power to command it we are forced to obey. And so when its impulses move us, none of us can stop their sudden promptings from easily breaking out, and even more easily overflowing into words which are the ever-ready indications of the heart's emotions... I will therefore hold my hand from writing words which I cannot restrain my tongue from speaking; would that a grieving heart would be as ready to obey as a writer's hand!'"

And she never addresses him in an intimate way again."

Sadness peered through Lily's eyes, and Sara leaned over to give her a hug.

"It looks like it's going to rain soon," Lily said. The sky was beginning to grow patches of charcoal over its former cerulean expanse. "Come on, let's find your apple orchard."

Lily and Sara located the proper approach. By then, a mystical thickness swelled the air. Thunder clouds rumbled ominously, and heavy, widely spaced drops of rain burst like tiny water balloons on their arms and shoulders. But they weren't ready to leave. Not yet. They wound their way through the matted lengths of unmowed grass, separately weaving among the natural umbrella of the older trees. Lily could almost feel Cheryl and Gil peering at them from some timeless space where they waited for Sara to bring them to life upon a page; the same timeless space where Heloise and Abelard, still young and unmarked by the ravages of their fate, caressed each other in flickering firelight on an innocent Paris night.

CHAPTER 10

Confusion is a word we have invented
for an order which is not understood.

—Henry Miller

Julian's plane began its descent into La Guardia. He roused himself from the agitated heaviness that was as close as he had come to sleep, and fastened his seatbelt. The steward collected his empty wine cups and the hill of shredded napkins he'd mindlessly sculpted into a question mark.

Courting denial, at times Julian convinced himself he was making more of his encounter with Lily than was warranted. But then, without wanting to, he found himself recalling the lovely green of her eyes or how the right side of her mouth curled slightly more than the left when she smiled. Again he was seduced into questioning everything he'd counted on, every understanding that had once seemed reasonable and dependable.

The airport was crowded with people and the

congestion seemed to bring out the worst in them. Julian wondered how this madness could have appeared normal to him three short months before. Now he felt more at home with the spirited songs of cardinals and chickadees, with the hypnotic dance of tumbling water, with long stretches of green. He had only needed a carry-on, so at least he didn't have to fight the frenzy at the baggage claim. Getting a taxi, however, took some maneuvering.

"Ninety-second and Riverside," Julian said as he got in. For a moment, he'd almost given his and Sam's old address. The traffic was considerable, five o'clock rush hour, and Julian was in no mood for the superficial conversation the driver tried to engage him in.

"If you don't mind me saying so, you look like you had a lousy trip. You live heeah?" the cabby asked, revealing his Brooklyn roots. He was the stereotypical native New York taxi driver, an abrasive and dying breed.

"No," Julian replied.

There was a time when Julian hadn't wanted to live anywhere else, a time New York had been the perfect, drab camouflage for the purer colors of himself he hadn't been ready to reveal.

"So, you here on business, or what?"

"Visiting friends." Julian tried not to encourage the exchange.

"C'mon lady, you got plenty of room!" the driver shouted, as if the woman attempting to switch lanes could hear him. "Worst time of day for driving in from the airport."

"Thanks for reminding me," Julian said, mostly to himself.

The taxi finally pulled up in front of the restored brownstone overlooking the Hudson River, which Evan and Marc, Julian and Sam's oldest friends, called home. They wouldn't be there yet, but they were expecting Julian, and he still had a key.

Julian let himself in and stood for a while testing the environment. The living room looked the same—the inviting arrangement of creamy, contemporary furniture, the richly patterned Oriental rugs, Evan's collection of hand-blown glass—yet it felt different. Before, the air had shaped itself around him. He fit into it like a puzzle piece. Now, he seemed to be hovering on its perimeter with no space carved out for his new, unfamiliar contours.

Julian brought his bags up to the guest room, then came down and sank his stressed body into the sofa. Here, in New York, he could almost forget Lily. He could almost forget the unreal feelings that spilled onto his canvases and confused his heart. In New York, missing Sam took priority. A collage of him formed in Julian's thoughts—the little notes he often left taped to the bathroom mirror, the way his cheeks flushed when he fluffed the punch line to a joke, how he cajoled Julian into midnight outings to eat cappuccino ice cream in a chocolate waffle cone. When it hurt too much to remember anything more, Julian fell into a deep sleep. He woke an hour later to the tumble of a lock.

"Julian! God it's good to see you. Let me look at you." Evan ran a loving eye over his friend's frayed demeanor, then threw his arms around him. "You don't look so hot, Juls. But we'll fix that. Some food, talk, maybe a good cry and you'll be better than new."

Marc walked over and embraced Julian. "We've missed you."

"I've missed you, too. Both of you. Very much."

Marc looked at his watch. "It's seven-thirty. You must be famished. Do you feel like going out or should we throw something together here?"

"Whatever you guys want to do is fine with me."

"There's a new place on 10th," Evan said. "Italian. Nothing fancy, but everyone says the food is wonderful."

"Italian sounds great," Julian replied. He'd gotten a second wind.

Julian looked hard at Marc. Then at Evan. He was sure they all felt Sam beneath the silence. There were years of history among them, years of sharing their love of art and food, of supporting each other through struggle and sorrow, of crying and laughing together at a world whose perspective was so unlike their own.

"So how long can you stay?" Marc said.

"I have to see Elgin at the gallery tomorrow, and then I need to get back."

"Then we'd better make the most of it," Evan added. "Starting with food. I'm starving."

"Me, too," Julian replied.

Mia Rosa's, an informal, family run establishment, prided itself on impeccable ingredients, and recipes passed down through four generations of Merullos. When Julian and his friends arrived, the entry foyer already had several parties waiting, but they were all seated within ten minutes. The three of them were escorted to a corner table in a small room to the left of the main dining area. The atmosphere felt intimate, with comfortably low lighting and the mellow glow of a candle at each table. A wide, chair-rail molding ran a little below the center of the walls with matching walnut paneling below it. The area above was painted in a soft, pale peach and decorated with colorful framed posters of the great Italian operas—*Aida, Tosca, Madame Butterfly, La Traviata*. Copen blue linen covered the tables.

Julian did not talk as much as usual during dinner. For one thing, he was enjoying the array of textures and aromas before him. He dipped warm, crusty Italian bread in rosemary-infused olive oil, and savored his shrimp scampi in white garlic sauce, which was served over hand-made linguini. He hadn't fixed himself a decent meal in months. But mostly, Julian was waiting for just the right pearls to string into words, just the right language to speak what was beyond language, what might never come out of his mouth the way he felt it in his heart. He was sure Evan and Marc could tell he had something difficult to say. He was grateful they knew him well enough not to pry, that they understood he'd talk when he was ready.

"So, how do you like living in the mountains?" Marc said.

"I actually like it more than I expected."

"Do you miss the city?" Evan said.

"Sometimes, but not as much as I thought I would. But I do miss you guys."

"We talk all the time about how much we miss you,"

Marc said. "And Sam."

"If he were here now," Evan said, "he'd probably be eating calamari or scungilli or some other slimy thing, watching me make faces at him, teasing me about my culinary cowardice."

"He probably would." Julian felt wistful. His eyes drifted into memory. His throat tightened. He lifted his wine glass. "To Sam."

"The best," Marc said.

"The Dom Perignon of a mostly Gallo world," Evan added.

They drank to Sam.

"So, Julian," Marc began, his tone obviously attempting to lift the mood, "any gallery connections?"

"I went to dinner with some people in Asheville whom Elgin introduced me to, and it's possible I might have a show in the fall or winter."

"That's great, Juls!" Evan said.

Marc smiled. "Maybe we'll come down for your opening."

"We're talking Asheville, North Carolina here, not New York City. This is small scale news."

"So you're saying you don't want us to come," Marc teased.

"Anytime, guys. You know that." Julian turned to Marc. "What's going on with you? How's the show going?"

Evan interrupted. "I wouldn't be surprised if this guy of ours gets nominated for a Tony. He's a lighting genius!"

Marc reached over and affectionately stroked Evan's arm. "Not so fast. Nothing's happened yet, but I'm being optimistic. I feel pretty good about the work on this play."

"I can't think of anyone I would be happier for," Julian said. "I'll be rooting for you. And what about you Ev? Haven't you been teaching some new course?"

"You mean 'The Gay Male Voice in Literature'?"

"Yeah."

"The semester's almost over, but it's been going really well. Of course that might be because half of my students are gay and the other half are women."

"Why do you think so many women are drawn to take a course like that?" Julian asked.

"Because Evan is so irresistible," Marc teased.

"We gay men are always irresistible to women," Evan said.

Julian's stomach lurched. Ever since he'd noticed such things, women had been attracted to him. That was what led him to his first and only heterosexual experience. That, and rumors of his homosexuality. He was in high school, pretending, for his parent's sake, to be something he was not. Called "adorable" with "a great body," he found it difficult to continually make excuses to the girls who flaunted themselves in front of him. And deathly afraid the rumors about him would get back to his father, he began dating a girl named Monica. Awkwardly he moved through the bases with her—or more accurately, she moved through the bases with him—until they'd finally "done it." Soon afterwards, and much to his relief, Monica broke up with him.

"Anybody want dessert?" Marc signaled to the waiter.

They all passed, and Marc ordered coffee. By the time it was served, Julian was ready to disclose his experiences of the last months. "I want to tell you some things that have been going on with me, but I want you to promise to hear me out without interrupting or I might not be able to say it all. Okay?"

"Sure," they both said.

Over their third round of refills, Evan and Marc were caught up on the bizarre details of Julian's recent life—paintings of castrated monks and cathedral spires, meeting Lily and being recognized from a dream, a possible reincarnational drama, potential madness. But Julian saved the hardest part for last.

"I have feelings for Lily I can't cubbyhole. I don't know where they belong, how to fit them in. I don't even know how to talk about them."

"Just say it, Juls," Evan said.

"I don't know what I believe about this Abelard and Heloise stuff, but I *am* pulled toward her in some very deep way. I may even love her. I don't understand any of it."

"Are you trying to say you're sexually attracted to her?" Evan said.

Julian paused, squirmed in his chair. "No. At least I don't think so. That's part of the confusion. I've known I was gay since I was eleven years old. It's who I am. But I feel something here that goes beyond sexual preference, something deeper than what a body can express. Does that make any sense to you, Ev?"

"I confess Juls, this is a hard one to grasp, but I'm stretching. Why didn't you tell her you're gay?"

"I couldn't. I could sense her feelings—for me—and I knew she would have been crushed. The irony of it is, so would I. I think I would have been crushed if she had pushed me away."

Evan stared at Julian as if trying to take in the finer meaning of what he was saying.

"I know all of this sounds ludicrous. I've been over it a thousand times in my mind. I mean I hardly even know Lily, and she already tugs at my heart." Julian turned to Marc. "So what do you think?"

"I think denial is an insidious thing, Julian. You have to tell her you're gay before it gets way out of hand. I think all the cards have to be laid on the table before either of you can know where any of this might be going."

"I know. I've sort of left her with the idea I might be interested. I've been living like a recluse—physically isolated, mentally fragmented, emotionally confused." Julian's eyes clouded over. "Shit! Why did Sam have to die and leave me at the mercy of a woman."

CHAPTER 11

Now by this moon, before this moon shall wane
I shall be dead or I shall be with you...

—Edna St. Vincent Millay
Fatal Interview

When he returned from New York, Julian called Lily. "I want to see you," he said. "I need to see you, Lily. There are things I must tell you—important and difficult things."

At the sound of his voice, the phone grew heavy in Lily's hand. Her pulse ran off in a hundred ghostly directions.

"You can come over this evening, if you like," she said. "I'll make tea."

Julian had finally called, yet some nuance in the way he spoke caused Lily to contemplate the worst. Maybe he was coming to tell her he never wanted to see her again. Or that he thought she was deranged. Or that there's a wife and three kids. Or—Oh God, please not this!—that he's a priest or a monk yet again, and hadn't known how to tell her. An hour later, however, when Lily saw Julian standing at her threshold, her anxiety was momentarily abated in his smile.

They entered the living room, and, as if frozen in time, stood very still, facing each other. Without language, without reason, a palpable passion grew between them. The room became luminous. Lily was about to break all her intuitive rules of questing and waiting. She had failed to become the one-who-waits. If she did not touch Julian right then, she would dissolve into a trillion dots of dust there in front of him. Whatever it was he had come to tell her must be put off for just a while. She would not let anything destroy this moment.

Julian had every intention of telling Lily the truth, yet there, in her presence, he wasn't at all certain what that was. Could something have changed so completely within him that he might desire a woman? He was terrified to find out. If he lost his sexual identity, an identity he had fought so hard to make peace with, who would he be? What would be left of him? No. He did not think he desired Lily in that way, and yet, he found himself about to let his mouth meet hers.

Slowly, Lily moved toward Julian, her eyes locked into his. He hesitated briefly, but did not resist, and she met him in a kiss, savoring the ancient jasmine that swirled around them.

What am I doing? Julian's mind tumbled inside him. He had made love with a woman only that one time, very long ago, and mostly out of fear and denial. *I could stop this in an instant. I could speak now and prevent inevitable disaster.*

Yet he did not. Instead, he let himself be seduced by the moment, by Lily, by the memory of something so deep it rode the silence between unspoken syllables. He felt Lily take his hand and gently guide him toward her bedroom. Unsure of how to embrace or reject what was happening, he moved on the surface of it—not fully immersed, yet not totally separate. He longed to be touched again, to be held. And some part of him was pulled toward Lily with a force he couldn't explain, as if choice wasn't even an option.

Lily stepped out of her dress. She found herself wishing there was more of her to give to Julian—fuller breasts, more rounded hips, longer hair. She could almost feel how Abelard must have gently unraveled Heloise's waist-long braid, raked his fingers sensually through the thick waves. Lily watched as Julian removed his sweater and jeans, draped them over a chair and slid onto the bed in just his underwear. She saw only perfection, and he was almost too beautiful—the smooth curve of his shoulder, his softly sculpted arms and chest. Lily ached to touch him. She slid into bed next to him, slipped the covers over them. They each shimmied out of their underwear.

Throwing inhibition to the wind, Lily danced her fingers and lips over him, deliberately, tenderly, resting upon each warm and pulsing place. She didn't care that Julian didn't return her gifts. In fact, she hardly noticed. When Lily could no longer contain what reverberated through her, she opened to receive his exquisite richness. Their bodies intimately joined, Lily longed to become one heartbeat, one breath.

But it did not happen.

Orgasmic release was not enough. The deeper

communion they each yearned for seemed to hover just beyond, as if a cosmic circuit had not been able to be completed. They held each other, both acutely aware of what had not occurred. Each sensed that something subtle, yet so vital was missing.

Julian was certain his sexual preference had not miraculously changed, but what it meant to him was no longer easily defined. What he found he now desired was more than just another man. It was Lily in a man's body. He wanted Lily's sensibilities, Lily's heart, Lily's soul in the right energetic circuitry to spark his own. He couldn't explain why, but just as he'd instantly known with Sam, Julian knew he loved Lily. Yet he also knew he wouldn't let this kind of intimacy happen again. He could never again pretend he was something he was not.

Lily and Julian lay together waiting for a sign from heaven. Disappointment and embarrassment thickened their air. Lily fought back tears with every breath. If she had been able to look at her lover's face, she would have seen his battle had been lost. Julian sat up and swept a tear from his cheek. Then, without knowing what might actually come out, he spoke.

"Maybe it has something to do with this Abelard business," he began softly, and with obvious strain, "but I've often had the vague and inexplicable feeling there was a price a man must pay for loving a woman. Maybe that's why I was born with a body drawn to loving men."

Lily couldn't mistake what Julian had just confessed, and he might as well have stabbed her through. Her sobs were sudden and quiet and deep. This was one thing she had not anticipated. Even hearing he was a priest or a monk would have been a thousand times kinder. At least, she thought, that was surmountable. There were options, possibilities. But homosexuality? For her, that had the finality of castration. Julian's words shut the window of her heart seemingly forever, bolted it as tight as any convent door, and she was suffocating.

"Lily, I'm so sorry. This is all my fault." In his thirty-nine years, Julian had never felt so raw and fragile. "I let things get out of hand. Can you ever forgive me?"

Trembling, Lily jumped out of bed and slipped on a T-shirt. A glacier froze itself fully formed at her center. "Please leave."

"There are things I need to explain. Can't we talk a little?"

"No. You've explained enough. Please go."

Lily left the room as Julian began to dress. If she watched him now, saw how his hair fell boyishly onto his brow, studied the seductive curve of his back as he slipped into his jeans, the ice might begin to melt and she would have to feel what was roiling beneath it.

When Julian came out of the bedroom, he found Lily solemn and pale, a funereal flower, sitting on the couch. She glanced toward him struggling to maintain her icy stance in the warmth of his eyes.

"I'm leaving," Julian said. "But not without saying this."

Lily looked away in silence.

"It was never my intention to hurt you, and I don't know why I couldn't tell you about myself before it had gotten to this point, but I do know that despite whatever obstacles are between us, and, as impossible as it might sound, and, without having a clue as to what to do about it, I think I love you, Lily." With those words, Julian turned from her and left before she could see him lose whatever composure he had managed to muster.

For a few more moments, Lily remained still, frozen where she was. If she faced the sun now, she would soon run wild like a summer stream, and she didn't know what deep silt, jutting rocks or steep embankments she might have to negotiate. Finally, she got up and put the kettle on, but by the time Lily had poured tea, the ice broke apart, rumbled to the surface. Without thinking, she hurled the cup of hot liquid across the kitchen, porcelain smashing into pieces against the wall. "Oh God," she cried, "how can this be happening?"

CHAPTER 12

If I might spread soft words like living grass
Laid smooth beneath the heavy wheels of Time;
If I might loose the river of a rhyme
Or build a pavement out of gold and glass
Providing Heaven for you to walk upon,
It would be well; it would be better done.

—Elinor Wylie
A Red Carpet for Shelley

Too overwhelmed by what had transpired between them to know how to reach for each other, Lily and Julian turned to their art. Julian's grief and confusion slid across his canvas in a splash of new light. His paintings became visionary symphonies with richly textured hues and shimmering overlays that seemed to take on more dimensions than the medium could possibly allow. It was as if he was trying to translate onto his canvas the landscapes of the heart. For beneath each stroke, each line, each sweep of impossible color was the thought of Lily.

For Lily, only poetry could help ease her profound disappointment. Writing was the only way to transform her pain into at least some glimmer of light. This is what Yeats must have felt when Maude Gonne would not become his wife, Lily thought. What Elinor Wylie must have known intensely when, divided by a hundred years, Percy Bysshe Shelley haunted her heart. This terrible aching emptiness that compels one to write.

Lily's devastating loneliness spun into poetry at a dizzying pace. For a while, her unhappiness found a degree of fulfillment, her frustration, a measure of release. She felt she'd been waiting for Julian all her life, and in some deep way every sentence she'd ever written had been fueled by the longing for him. She wondered if longing was all there would ever be.

So, often roaming the pre-dawn hours when shadows tricked the senses and spirits hovered close urging a cerulean stroke or whispering lyric verse into the latent air, Julian painted, and Lily wrote her *Prayer to an Ancient God*:

> …How will it go this time?
> Will I be doomed again to endless misery
> for wanting something he can't give?
> I pray you, say there's hope in loving
> him. And if a larger purpose must be lived,
> enlighten me; help me make some sense
> of this insanity.

Prayers are always answered, and one night, Lily had a dream. She dreamed she had been left in the middle of the ocean enveloped by a dense fog and was frantically trying to stay afloat. Suddenly the fog cleared and she saw a brightly lit buoy on top of which Lovina, in the guise of a rather large angel, sat eating M&Ms. Despite her ample wings, Lily doubted she could have become easily airborne.

"Pssst, Lily," the angel said. "Come here. Have an M&M."

Lily swam over to the edge, cautiously eyeing the substantial apparition.

"I've been waiting for you." She adjusted her hovering halo, which had slipped to the left, making her look as if she'd consumed a bit too much ambrosia.

"Am I dead?" Lily asked.

"Goodness, no! You're dreaming. I knew you'd need me again once he found you."

"I wish he hadn't! I wish I'd never seen him! I wish the whole affair would go away!"

"Nonsense," the angel replied. "That's your small self talking. Actually, my dear, you've gotten exactly what you wished for."

"Are you telling me I wanted this?" Lily shouted.

"Yes. You both did. Both of you wanted a do-over."

"A what?"

"Uh oh." The angel paused as if she was hearing some urgent inside message. "Gotta fly," she said. "Call me!"

With that, she and the buoy vanished.

Lily woke suddenly, the details of her strange dream still spinning in her mind. The clock glowed 5:45. She was too tired to write anything down. Since that last devastating encounter with Julian, Lily had spent many candle-lit hours deep in tears and poetry. Or, comforted by the anonymity of darkness, she lounged on the patio, wondering how the impossible tangle of her relationship with Julian would ever unravel itself.

If he'd never entered my dreams, Lily thought, I wouldn't have known who he was. But knowing, how could I not look at him? And looking, how could I not want him? I am as wretched as Heloise.

For days she felt tenuous in the world, as if pieces of herself where scattered somewhere else, spinning out scenarios she could sense, yet had no direct recollection of. In a moment of great loneliness, she wondered if a life without Julian was even a life worth living. But a week had helped to blunt at least the sharpest edge of her pain, and, despite what might be happening in more rarefied realms, Lily knew she needed to pull herself back into everyday focus. She had a business to attend to, one she'd work hard to make a success. It was close to sunrise. If she tried to go back to sleep, it would be difficult to rouse herself again by 7:30. Instead, she showered, dressed, made tea, and walked onto the patio to greet the colors of morning. At 9:30 she headed downtown.

Maya had arrived at InWord Bound early, as she often did, and when Lily got there she found her assistant emptying the vase of wilted gladioli.

"Morning," Lily said.

"Hi, Lily."

"I'll bring some fresh flowers tomorrow, if you'll

remind me before I leave."

"Will do."

"Maya, I just want you to know how much I appreciate you around here. Thanks for bearing with my erratic moods these last months. I'll make it up to you. You know I've been dealing with some personal issues."

Lily had shared with Maya only enough of the events of her impossible love life to explain the moments of teariness and depression she had difficulty hiding. Maya seemed always to respect her privacy.

"It's fine, Lily. I'm very good at handling the unexpected."

"Only one of the things you're very good at." Lily smiled.

Maya picked up a stack of used paperbacks that were ready to be shelved.

"I'll do that," Lily said. She felt like involving herself in something that would leave her alone with her thoughts. "Do you mind staying up front instead?"

"Sure."

"Thanks."

Lily took the books from Maya, and headed toward the shelves along the far side wall. She felt ghostly, an apparition of the Lily she had been before. Before dreams. Before Lovina. Before Julian. The emptiness left by Julian's confession seemed so vast, at times she felt she might fall into it and be lost forever. Poof! Gone! She thought it perhaps a kinder demise than the living death of seemingly irreparable heartbreak.

Shifting the focus back to her work, Lily continued placing the books alphabetically by author. As she squeezed the last paperback, John Irving's *A Prayer for Owen Meany,* into the *i's,* Lily sensed someone moving toward her. She turned to see who it was. Lovina sauntered down the aisle, stopping to glance at something that had caught her eye. Maya trailed behind.

"Lily, look who's here!" Maya said.

Lily should have been used to her dreams walking into her waking life, but she was not. She was certain, however, that except for the wings and halo, it had been Lovina she'd encountered in the middle of that ocean.

"Lovina." Lily managed a polite but strained smile. She could feel a wave building in the pit of her stomach.

Lovina embraced her. "Have you had any unusual visions lately?" she inquired, confirming Lily's bizarre suspicions.

"It looks like you two might have something to talk about," Maya said, "so I'll just go back to my work." She walked away humming.

Lily felt surreal. "As a matter of fact," she confessed, "I have had a rather strange encounter."

"I thought so," Lovina said.

This is too weird, Lily thought. But she wanted to believe in Lovina, to believe that somehow Lovina held the wisdom to make sense of things that seemed senseless.

Lovina wedged the book she had purchased from Maya into her large, over-stuffed bag. After digging around for a moment, she pulled out a purple card with silver writing. "Well, my dear, I really must be off. Let me give you one of my new cards." She handed it to Lily. It read: *LOVINA—a buoy of clarity in the turbulent sea of confusion.*

"Call me," she echoed from the dream.

Lily watched Lovina hurry off. "I will," she replied, but Lovina had already flown out the door.

C H A P T E R 13

Only three things are infinite: the sky in its stars, the sea in its drops of water, and the heart in its tears.

—Gustav Flaubert
to Louise Colet

"It's called indicolite," Lovina said.

Lily had been eyeing the jeweled pendant that rested in the hollow between Lovina's collarbones.

"A rare kind of tourmaline," Lovina continued. "Especially useful to wear when you want to stay in the divine heart."

"It's lovely." Lily had noticed the stone before. Deep teal blue, like Julian's eyes.

Lily was seated across from Lovina at the mahogany dining table, a glass of water on a round coaster in front of each of them. The late morning sun shone through one of the opened windows casting a wide ribbon of light over a hanging fuchsia plant with its cascade of magenta and purple blooms.

Lovina turned toward Egypt, India and Peru who were lined up and purring beside her chair. "If you're ready, we can begin."

Lily wasn't sure if Lovina was talking to her, or to the feline familiars, who, in unison, ceased their purring and rearranged themselves in an arc around Lovina's legs. "I guess I'm ready."

Lily had given much thought to all that transpired since she'd last visited with Lovina, and how Lovina had been right about many things. She certainly had become involved in "no ordinary love affair." And she certainly felt an intensity that tipped any reasonable scale of emotion. Looking into Lovina's pale green eyes, Lily recalled her recent dream, and how the "angel" or whoever it was, seemed to be telling her she had *chosen* to become involved with Julian, that it was what she'd wanted. But why? What possible gain had come of it? All it had led to was disappointment and betrayal.

"I think we can forego the M&M's," Lovina said, sweeping aside the half-empty candy dish, as if trying to move it out of the way of temptation.

"Yes. That's fine." Lily wasn't in the mood for any psychic subterfuge anyway.

"I know you have many questions, my dear, but let me begin by telling you that the essence of the relationship you've come here to talk about remains at the center of everything that matters. And I will also tell you there appear to be future connections for both of you, relationships that are separate from the one you have with each other. While on a scale of emotional intensity from one to ten I've called your current encounter a seventeen, the possibility exists for an involvement at a more manageable eight or nine."

"I can't even entertain the thought of any other relationship."

"Of course, dear. I understand. Let's deal with what's happening now."

Lily took a sip of water. Her hand trembled slightly. "I'm not sure what's real anymore. I feel the presence of a nun who's been dead for eight hundred years, people are walking out of my dreams and into my bookstore, I'm passionately in love with a man who is not sexually attracted to women, and I've been seriously questioning whether or not I have any semblance of sanity left."

"Yes. Well, first of all, let me assure you that neither you nor...what is his name now? J. Something with a J."

" Julian?" Lily felt unsettled by the fact Lovina didn't know Julian's name.

"Yes. Neither you nor Julian is insane. There are many things happening here." Lovina took on a more purposeful air and formal inflection. "I'll try to give you an overview, and if you have questions or want to dialogue along the way, you can. All right?"

"Yes."

"Today we must be more serious," Lovina explained with a smile. "There are important things to say."

"Okay." Lily was comforted by this more focused side of Lovina, reassured that she knew what she was doing.

Lovina took a sip of water, paused slightly, then continued. "There comes a time in our soul's growth when we are asked to call upon the best of ourselves, to test ourselves, to ask ourselves—'How strong is my truth now?'" She closed her eyes every so often, as if it helped her more clearly focus on the impressions she was receiving. "That time of testing is upon you and Julian. It's what you wanted, what you knew you needed to face in this life. As Heloise and Abelard, many feelings were left unresolved, feelings you both, in part, still carry with you, even though—and this is important—your current relationship must stand on its own power in the present."

"Yes, I understand. But are you saying we *were* Heloise and Abelard, as in reincarnation?"

Peru looked up at Lovina and meowed loudly.

"Yes, I know," Lovina mumbled. She paused for a moment.

"Where were we?" she said.

"I was asking if you're saying Julian and I *were* Abelard and Heloise."

"Yes. That's the simplest way to put it. Have you not already come to this on your own?"

"I suppose. But what exactly does it mean?"

"In part, it means you each carry the soul energy and experiences of those individuals within what is best described as cellular memory. There are encodings that are triggered when you come together. You have a soul history—in this case a very old and deep one."

Lily felt her stomach contract forcing a timeless well of sadness to the surface.

"Because of what has been left unresolved, you and Julian have set up an opportunity to do it differently this time."

"I feel as if I've known him forever, and if I have, we must have had other opportunities. Why haven't we resolved this before?"

"Of course there were other lifetimes together, but this one now is pivotal. It's the one in which you both decided you were ready to face what neither of you before had the courage to look at."

Lily ran a hand through her hair. "I don't feel very courageous."

"But you are. In many lifetimes you and he saw each other only briefly in the physical, and even though there was recognition, the momentary stirring of the heart, you each had other things to do and chose to interact primarily in dreams where it would be less overwhelming. You can now understand why."

"He feels like my own soul. Sometimes it's like I want to become him. I don't know how else to put it."

"Yes, my dear. I understand. Let me see how I can explain. You can think of your deeper relationship as a mystic marriage. But unlike matrimony, which can last for many years or even decades, this larger coming together may, on this level, complete its purpose in a relatively short time. On a soul level, however, the bond is eternal. That's why there's an almost constant and overwhelming desire to be one. Even though in a body this is usually expressed sexually, it's a spiritual yearning, and within your chosen situation and obstacles, you have an ideal opportunity to begin to understand this in a different way than most. We don't get the largest challenge until we are ready, and it can feel like an explosion of every part of our being."

Lily felt close to tears. "I can't stop wanting to love him," she said.

"It doesn't mean you have to stop loving him. It

means you must find a larger way *to* love, a larger understanding of what love is—which has nothing to do with things like sexual preference. When truth stands at the door, do we open and let it in, or do we deny it? That is the question." Lovina passed her a box of tissues.

Lily took one, but didn't use it. "Why did he have to be gay?"

"That's what he felt he needed to experience in this lifetime, partly because of his particular fears. If he wasn't gay, it's very possible he would have had great difficulty allowing himself to trust love in any form. Any kind of resolution would have again been impossible. Try to think of this in the largest sense, my dear."

"I guess I can see how being gay might have given him a certain measure of safety between us," Lily said. She sipped her water. "Especially if it's true he carries the memories of Abelard's experience."

"We are often put in a situation where the obstacles seem insurmountable, because that's the only place that has real meaning, the place where we must risk everything—being misunderstood, being rejected, losing friendships, failing, being thought mad...everything. One of the hardest things is to be honest in the face of massive dishonesty. Do you understand this?"

"Maybe a little. I don't know."

"In time things will become clearer."

"I hurt so much."

"I know, my dear." Lovina closed her eyes and continued. "Once I was asked, 'what is unconditional love?' The best answer I could give was the love that cannot be denied, because when love is understood for what it is, and when it is unconditional, it cannot be denied. Whatever obstacles exist do not matter."

For a moment, a chord in Lily resounded with meaning, but lesser sounds pulled her back to her pain. "I still don't understand why we would have chosen to go through this kind of humiliation."

"You didn't choose humiliation. You created an experience that you have labeled humiliation. The only meaning anything has is what we give it. You and Julian agreed to come together in order to give yourselves an opportunity to heal what has left each of you, in your own way, emotionally cloistered. A larger destiny brought you together, but what happens as a result is not pre-ordained."

"I feel like I'm the one who blew it, that if I had followed my instinct to wait, and allowed Julian to speak before I..."

Images of that wrenching evening flooded Lily's memory—the way she'd practically thrown herself at Julian, the uninhibited way she'd made love to him, his confession. She began to weep.

Lovina looked at her with great tenderness. "You did what was in your heart to do. And Julian chose his own response, for more reasons than he can consciously understand. It's all right, my dear. There are no mistakes in this."

"I feel so embarrassed."

"I understand."

"How could I not have sensed from the beginning that he was gay?"

"You created Julian to be what you wanted and needed him to be."

"How?"

"It's what happens in relationships. Often, we take what we see and because our small self thinks it *needs* something from another, we create in our minds a person who, in reality, may not exist."

"What are you saying, that Julian doesn't exist?" Lily wanted to be sure Lovina was speaking metaphorically, and that all that had happened in the last months had not been one gargantuan hallucination.

"No, my dear. He is very real. Can you understand what I'm saying?"

"I think so. I admit I did see Julian as I hoped he would be, not necessarily as he was. And because my feelings for him were so deep, I saw the best, the largest of him. It didn't occur to me that might not be the way he sees himself."

"Many times, that's the case."

"Is that what happened with Heloise and Abelard? Did Heloise grieve an entire lifetime for the loss of a man who didn't exist?"

"You're beginning to see many things."

"So Heloise continued to imagine what might have been with the Abelard she'd fallen in love with, a very different man from the one he later felt himself to be."

"Yes." Lovina continued. "Abelard's 'misfortune,' as he called it, affected him very deeply, and he judged himself harshly for loving Heloise in the way he did. He came to feel he'd been justly punished for his sins. He couldn't have allowed himself to think of what he'd set in motion in any other way and go on with his life."

"So he just abandoned Heloise for twelve years?" Lily

uncrossed, then re-crossed her legs, the right one now bobbing against the left.

"From Abelard's perspective, my dear, he had not deliberately abandoned her. He'd acted out of as much human love as he was capable of feeling—which, in truth, was far less than Heloise had chosen to believe. He did what he thought best for the Heloise of *his* vision. Each of them defined love differently, interpreting it through their own needs and limitations and conditions."

"This is so complicated, Lovina."

"I know it feels that way. You've allowed yourself the gift of Julian so you could finally face and move through matters you've refused to look at for a very long time. In this life, you've been very cautious when it's come to love, often afraid to follow your heart."

Lily knew Lovina was right. Ever since feeling rejected by Alex all those years before, she'd resigned herself to keeping her heart protected at all cost. At least, until Julian. And look at the price she was paying for *that*.

"You've carried the feeling that expressing passion leads only to tragedy," Lovina continued, "that you will be judged and shamed for it. Now you must stop punishing yourself. How it will play out this time, with Julian, and what it will ultimately mean for you and for him cannot be predetermined. It has yet to be lived. And it may involve experiences and choices you're not even aware of at this point. I don't expect you to grasp all of this yet, my dear, but you will."

Lily felt tired and overwhelmed. "What do I do now?"

"He's told you how he feels about you, and you can trust that. The waiting you were sensing you needed to do is no longer necessary. He's now waiting for you. Go to him and open your heart to him. With no conditions. And no expectations. That is the true challenge. Lovina then removed the blue jewel from around her neck. "I'm told this is now to be yours," she said, and, in the spirit of a generosity far beyond material measure, she reached across the table and passed it to Lily.

CHAPTER 14

May-be one is now reading this who
knows some wrong-doing of my past life...

—Walt Whitman
Leaves of Grass

Lily fondled the indicolite necklace that hung almost weightlessly around her neck. The antithesis of a certain crucifix, she thought. She'd worn it to work that day, and she smiled remembering how Maya had been able to give her a complete dissertation on the properties of its particular kind of tourmaline. She also made a point of telling Lily it had probably cost quite a bit. Whether or not such a thing held the power to keep a person in the "divine heart," or what exactly that was, Lily didn't know. But, besides the fact it was an elegant piece of jewelry, she figured it couldn't hurt to have a thing close by that might carry some degree of magic.

The session with Lovina left Lily with more questions than it answered. She still wondered who the "spirits" with whom Lovina communicated were. And who, exactly, Lovina was. And if there was really such a thing as a mystic marriage. And how one tests the strength of truth.

As she contemplated these uncertainties, Lily walked through her mundane chores. She picked up an empty teacup from the coffee table and carried it to the sink, put the skirt she had left draped over the bedroom chair on a hanger and hung it in the closet, gathered socks and underwear and dropped them into the laundry hamper in the bathroom. Her experiences these past months had been inexplicable, yet she couldn't deny the validity of them. She couldn't say they weren't real, that they didn't happen because they didn't fit into ordinary perception. Maybe mystery was all there was, and figuring things out was just a way to fool the part of herself that pretended to be in control. Maybe hardly anything was in anyone's control in the way she'd once thought.

Lily wondered what might have played out between them if Julian had not been gay. She wanted to believe he would have been able to acknowledge her and love her truly and freely, the way she imagined Heloise and Abelard had in their youth. She wanted to believe he, too, would have felt the ancient ember that still glowed between them, that together they would have been able to fan it into a new light. But she felt it more likely Lovina was right. If Julian hadn't been gay, he probably would have been too afraid to feel the kind of love a deeper part of him believed had once been his undoing. The moment he met her eyes, he probably would have turned away, cloistered himself in denial and again justified never looking back.

Lily noticed that the lilac pillar candle next to the box

of tissues on her night table was just about burned out. She took what was left of it from its brass holder and threw it in the waste basket. She made a mental note to replace it. She liked the scent of lilac near her bed. It reminded her of the fragrant bushes that grew beneath the windows at her grandmother Mia's house when she was a child, how she used to tell Lily "sweet smells bring sweet dreams."

About to lift the ceramic lamp in order to dust beneath it, Lily noticed something sticking out from underneath its base. When she tipped it back, she saw a folded square of paper. Without even touching it, Lily could feel Julian. There was no mistaking that sensation. She slid it tentatively into her hand, afraid to open it, afraid not to. She was certain it had been placed there after the wonder and horror of that night almost two weeks before, probably while she was frozen on the living room sofa and he was still dressing. She remembered it had seemed like an eternity until he'd finally come out.

Lily unfolded the note and glanced at it. She was trembling, a sense of foreboding churning in her gut. Her mind jammed, and the words and sentences on the page blurred into incomprehensible black on white marks. Slowly, they began to clear. *Dear Lily,* she read. *I am so...*

The phone rang, startling Lily. She found herself quickly refolding the note, slipping it back beneath the lamp for safe-keeping, as if its great and private secret needed to be protected even from a distant voice. Lily grabbed the phone on the fourth ring, right before she knew the machine would pick up.

"Hi," Sara said.

Sara's birthday! Lily had been busy at the shop all day

and forgot to phone when she'd gotten home. "I was just about to call you." Lily needed to cover her guilt. She tried to sound cheerful. "Happy happy birthday!"

"Thanks, Lily."

"So how does it feel to be forty-five?"

Sara laughed. "So far, about the same as forty-four."

Lily's mind was preoccupied with the note, and talking even to Sara at that moment felt like a struggle." That's reassuring. Did you do anything special today?"

Lily only caught fragments of Sara's reply—"decadent brunch with…pedicure…new bracelet…"

"Sounds wonderful."

"It was. So how are you doing?"

"Let's not talk about me," Lily said. Besides it being Sara's day, Lily was afraid if she told about the note, Sara might try to convince her to open it right then, and she felt she needed to face whatever it might say alone, and in her own way. "You listen enough to my sorry stories."

"There were plenty of times when our positions were reversed. Remember?" Sara said.

Lily remembered. Especially the time Sara was struggling to give up cigarettes. And also when she'd needed Lily's support during the emotional fiasco with Jean-Paul.

"I'm happy to be able to listen to your stories, Lil."

"Thanks, Sara, but I think I'll let things rest tonight, okay?"

"Of course."

"We're still on for lunch tomorrow, my treat, right?" Lily said.

"Sure."

"I have a little surprise for you I've been saving for weeks." It was a signed copy of one of Sara's favorite books, which had come into the shop—Lee Smith's, *Fair and Tender Ladies*.

"I like surprises." Sara paused. She seemed to sense Lily's reticence to talk. "So I'll see you tomorrow, okay? I love you."

"I love you, too, Sara."

Lily hung up and immediately retrieved the folded paper. She sat down at the edge of the bed. She wondered how many times she and Julian had come into and gone out of each other's lives, what other imprints had been left on their souls. There must have been happier scenarios. Why couldn't she have come upon one of those? Lily stared at the obscurity in her hand. Was there anything Julian could have written that would change the humiliation and disappointment that was now her constant torment? Anything that could alter the hopelessness of their circumstance? Were there any words that could ever right an eight-hundred-year-old wrong?

Lily thought the memory of Julian's confession would echo in her forever. "Maybe that's why I was born with a body drawn to loving men." How, in that moment, she'd wanted to lash out at him, tell him how much she hated him. How she'd wanted to physically hurt him, to place her tight fingers around the seemingly insensitive throat out of which those words had come, to reach inside of him and rip his heart out, like it felt he had done to hers.

And, in the next moment, how horrified and ashamed she had become of the violent thoughts she would never act upon, but hadn't imagined lived within her. Instead, she built an iceberg at her center, numbing every feeling, at least until Julian had removed his achingly beautiful self from her house.

Now Lovina was telling her to go to him, that he waited for her, that she could trust his feelings for her. But how in the world could she call him after what had happened between them? What could she say? How could she ever face him again? Maybe it was best just to let the whole encounter fade into oblivion, to forget Julian (was that even a possibility?), to ban him from her dreams, to go forward with her life.

Lily put the note in the pocket of her jeans. She needed to distract herself from the spinning at her center. She went into the kitchen and put on the kettle, then reached for the jar of chamomile teabags on the shelf above the counter. She took out a favorite mug with brightly colored grapes and berries painted over a pale yellow glaze. It had often calmed her spirits to drink from it. When the water boiled, Lily filled the cup and brought it to the dining room table. She removed the note from her pocket and placed it in front of her. She sat. She sipped her tea. And finally ready to face what Julian had to say, she unfolded the paper.

Dear Lily,

I am so so sorry. There's no excuse or explanation I can offer for why I couldn't tell you about myself earlier. Since I met you, I've understood nothing about my feelings. But I do know that it would deeply grieve me if you disappeared from my life. If you can find it in your heart to forgive my unforgivable behavior I will be waiting for you.

Love,
Julian

The words were written in an artist's fine uniform print, all capitals, except for Julian's name, which was signed. Lily stared at them until again they blurred into meaningless lines and spaces. She felt numb. She took another sip of tea, then, needing physical distance from the proximity of Julian's imprint, she got up and walked outside. She stood for a minute, watching the steady brightness of Venus in the flickering sky. "What now?" she whispered. Pacing the perimeter of the patio, she bent to nip several dead petunias from a basket she hadn't yet hung. And then, with the ache of centuries, Lily cried.

She cried for what had hardly been and what could never be. She cried because Julian still waited for her. She cried for the love she found the courage to feel. She cried for the dreams she had found and lost and found again. She cried because she felt alive in her pain. Lily cried long and deep because she knew she would never cry like this over anyone again.

And when she was finished crying, Lily called Julian.

CHAPTER 15

I will whisper something into the ear of your heart...

—Ellen Louisa Tucker
to Ralph Waldo Emerson

Atop a large, smooth boulder jutting into the stream at an edge of the Botanical Gardens, Lily and Julian faced the sun.

"I come here sometimes when I need a little natural magic," Lily said.

Julian smiled.

Their granite island was one of several accessible by climbing down the gravel path around the gardens, stepping carefully across smaller rocks. In front of them the swiftly moving current glistened in the late morning sun. Lily and Julian sat quietly watching. Several minutes passed before they began to test the deeper waters that had again carried them to each other.

"I'm glad you called," Julian said. He'd known the past couple of weeks had been *his* time to wait, to give Lily a space in which to sort out her feelings, to see if she could even bear to see him again.

"Me, too." Lily avoided Julian's eyes, afraid she'd again fall under his spell. She removed her shoes and socks and let her feet slip into the tumbling stream. "It's freezing!" she said, shivering.

Julian tested the temperature with his hand. Lily noticed the way the tendons fanned gracefully from his wrists to the base of his fingers. A tiny fleck of violet paint stained one of his nails.

"You're a brave soul," he said, rubbing his fingers together to warm them.

"Not so brave." Lily was thinking of more cowardly things—like how much she was holding back from caressing Julian's cheek, how futile their whole situation seemed, how sorry she felt for herself. She pulled her numb feet out of the water and let them dry on the sun-warmed stone. "So what brought you to the mountains?" She realized she knew almost nothing about Julian's former life.

"I lost my partner, Sam, about nine months ago. He died of cancer."

Lily let her eyes meet Julian's. "I'm so sorry," she said, her stomach contracting in the sudden awareness that Julian had a history of love and loss and a million other things of which she knew nothing and had been no part.

"I couldn't stay in New York after that. The void Sam left was too big to rattle around in alone. I was pretty much dead myself for a while."

"How long were you and Sam together?" Lily struggled to find compassion for Julian's loss. The knot in her stomach, however, tugged with jealousy.

"Seven years."

"I was married to Michael for nine. We divorced a few years ago."

"What happened?"

"You know the scene in *Moonstruck* where the moon is huge and full and everyone becomes intoxicated with romance?" Lily began.

"Sure."

"Well, the only thing that intoxicated Michael was the compulsion to analyze why the moon could not logically be that large, at that time of night, in that position in the sky."

"Got it." Julian laughed.

Lily felt herself easing back into some degree of comfort. "Besides his lack of poetry," she continued, "Michael was a nice guy and I did love him. Although I always felt something was missing, that I was waiting for something I couldn't define, but would know when it appeared."

"And has it…appeared?"

"Right out of a dream."

Julian wished he hadn't opened up that subject, and didn't take it any further.

"I'm hopelessly in love with you, you know." There, Lily had said it.

"I don't think love is ever hopeless." Julian recognized his words as those Sam might have used.

You're not the woman in this situation, Lily wanted to remind him, but instead kept to her confession. "Julian, I want you to know I wasn't only angry at *you* that night at my house." Just speaking about the unspeakable encounter made Lily queasy. "I was angry at myself. At my lack of timing, and my impatience, and my inappropriate actions. I certainly felt disappointment, but I was also deeply embarrassed. I've never seduced a man into my bed that way. I've never felt that kind of recognition or that depth of connection to anyone before. It took me over. I'm sorry for throwing you out so rudely."

"It was understandable." Julian picked up a pebble and threw it into the stream. "I'm sorry too, for not being honest with you sooner." He turned to Lily. "But what happened, happened—for whatever reasons. It can't be undone. And I need you to understand that it won't happen again. It didn't change the fact that I'm gay. So maybe it's best we put it to rest, okay?"

"After one question."

Julian eyed Lily cautiously. "What's that?"

"Did you mean what you said before you left? About loving me?" Lily needed to know.

Julian hesitated before answering, not sure how she might interpret his reply, not even sure what it meant for him. "Yes," he said.

It was the answer Lily had waited for, yet, where could they go from there? Mentally, she searched for a string of hope to hold onto, and found some loose threads. Chopin and George Sand were together nine years, even though, because of his illness, he was physically unable to make love. Heloise would have stayed with Abelard in a heartbeat if he had wanted it, even though they would not have been able to make love again. Or closer to the point—Dora Carrington and Lytton Strachey, despite their incompatible sexual orientation, not only shared a life, but often slept in the same bed without making love.

"There are people who are together and love each other," Lily found herself saying, "but for various reasons don't make love. People who are ill or..."

Julian didn't let her finish. "Or what? Castrated?"

Realities were bleeding into each other.

"I'm healthy, Lily. I have sexual needs and desires even if I don't choose to express them with someone I'm not in love with. Contrary to popular impression, not all gay men have impersonal, indiscriminate sex lives, especially not these days. And," Julian looked hard at Lily, "it's a new and difficult experience *not* to be sexually drawn to the person I *am* in love with. You think it's harder for you, but I think it's hard for both of us."

"I'm sorry, Julian. I don't even know how to talk about this." Lily wished she could take back what she'd said.

"I know." Julian calmed himself. "Forgive me. I didn't mean to snap at you. It's just that you don't know what it's like being gay. I've had to go through years of therapy to accept myself and even truly like myself, and I won't allow my sexual orientation to be made a defect in this. For me, it's your sexual packaging that's the obstacle. It works both ways."

"Yes. I can see that, Julian. I don't want to think of either of us as defective." Lily took a tissue from her pocket and blotted the few tears that had surfaced.

Julian attempted to shift the mood. "Do you want to walk a little?"

"That would be good."

As Lily leaned forward to tie her shoes, the indicolite necklace she was wearing unloosed itself from where it had been caught inside her shirt. Julian noticed it. "What is that?" he said. "It's exquisite."

"It's a kind of blue tourmaline called indicolite. A woman named Lovina gave it to me recently, sort of passed it on to me."

"Lovina?"

Julian gave Lily a hand up the steep embankment onto to the gravel path around the gardens. His touch coursed through her body, sending warmth to places she did not want it to. She held on a few seconds too long and felt Julian ease his fingers from hers.

"She's a psychic. I went to see her the other day." Lily wanted Julian to know. "She's a friend of my assistant, Maya's. I didn't know whether or not to tell you. How do you feel about such things?"

"I'm fine with it," Julian said, as they stopped to admire the rhododendrons, which had already opened in a sensuous profusion of purple, pink and white. They headed toward the gazebo. "It's not something I'm drawn to do myself right now, but I'd like to hear about it."

"Lovina claims we were Heloise and Abelard in another lifetime. She says at the soul level we have what she called a mystic marriage, and that we've set up a kind of test or opportunity to learn how to love in a larger way than just the physical." Lily waited for Julian to respond.

"Do you believe her?"

"I think I do. I had a dream about her, which, for me, added credibility. What do you think?"

"There's certainly something extraordinary going on

between us. I suppose what she says is possible. I'm trying to keep an open mind these days." Julian paused. "But did she gaze into her crystal ball and offer any predictions?" he teased.

Lily chuckled. "No. And it's M&Ms."

"What?"

"She uses M&Ms, not a crystal ball."

"O...kay." Julian was going to leave that little tidbit untouched.

"How it will turn out I'm afraid she says is up to us." Lily stroked the necklace. "She's the one who gave me this. It was hers."

For a moment, Julian drifted into himself.

"Am I losing you?" Lily was surprised by the broader implication of her words. These days she often didn't know what might come out of her mouth around Julian.

"No, but when you just mentioned Heloise and Abelard, I ...." Julian didn't finish. He was deciding whether or not to share what he was remembering. Meanwhile, he brought his attention back to Lily, put his arm around her. She melted into his side. "There's no reason we can't still embrace each other," he said. "Is there?"

"No, of course not."

The warmth of Lily against him felt comforting to Julian, but in a different way from what he was sure she felt. A person can die of not being touched, he often thought after Sam's death. They walked for a while in silence. Then—"Lily," he began.

"Yes?"

"There's an odd coincidence connected to this

Heloise and Abelard stuff I remembered a minute ago." Julian seemed to be speaking from a far off space. "And by telling you this, I'm not saying I necessarily believe it points to anything special."

Lily felt a wave of anxiety build in her solar plexus. "What is it?"

"Shortly after Sam and I met, we went to Paris together. We were so in love. Of course, we saw every great painting that could be crammed into our two weeks, but I also became obsessed with Notre Dame. I kept wanting to go back there. It held a fascination for me. A strange familiarity. I kept seeing overlapping visions of it in its different stages of completion, which is sometimes how it appears in my paintings, the ones I told you about in the café."

Lily's anxiety intensified. What Julian was saying seemed to put another crimp in so-called reality. They reached the gazebo and Lily slid onto a bench. Julian sat down next to her. They shifted to face each other, knees drawn to their chests like shields. Lily sifted every word Julian had spoken, especially "we were so in love."

Julian continued. "We also went with a Parisian friend, Nicole, to Père Lachaise cemetery to visit the grave of Oscar Wilde especially. Sam loved Wilde. It's an extraordinary place. Acres of park with wonderful old chestnut trees. Many great artists buried there—Balzac, Bizet, Chopin, Victor Hugo, Maria Callas, Gertrude Stein."

The name Père Lachaise made the hair on Lily's arms spike. She knew who else's final double resting place one could find there.

"Wilde's tomb was this huge contemporary sculpture. There were bouquets of fresh flowers piled around it's base, and little poems on small pieces of paper." Julian paused. Lily seemed far away. "This is probably boring you," he said.

"No, no. I'm listening. Please go on."

"Anyway, Nicole says, 'You two lovers have got to visit Heloise and Abelard,' and she takes us to their tomb explaining that they were moved there centuries after their deaths so they could lie together in the sarcophagus said to be Abelard's original. Then she..."

Lily interrupted. "The structure around it was built from the remains of The Paraclete, the monastery Abelard originally founded, where Heloise later became abbess."

Julian's eyes grew wide. "You know this?"

"Yes." Lily had already researched these things. She smiled. "So, go on."

"So, Nicole tells us a little about their sad and passionate history, the details of which it seems I'd conveniently forgotten. Or maybe repressed. As we're standing in front of their effigies, on the other side of the iron railing that surrounds the tomb, Sam, great romantic that he was, says, 'If these two ever come back, I hope they're able to do it differently.'"

Lily turned sharply toward Julian. "That's really what he said?"

"That's exactly what he said. Why?"

"Because what Lovina exactly said was, 'You and Julian have set up an opportunity to do it differently this time.'"

Julian ignored the implications in Lily's words. His

heart, at that moment, belonged to Sam. "There's one more small piece.

Lily turned away. "What's that?"

"It was Sam's wish that some of his ashes be carefully and discreetly scattered at Père Lachaise." Julian's voice caught in his throat. "He wanted at least a little of himself to rest in the company of so many who had left their creative imprint on the world." Julian paused, then went on as if in a reverie. "Several months ago, I, and our two closest friends, brought him there, and on a strange impulse, I went alone to the tomb of Heloise and Abelard. I was too consumed by grief to remember much of their story, only that Sam and I had stood there together. I circled the site with a little of Sam's ashes, letting them slip through my fingers. 'Like Heloise and Abelard,' I said to Sam, 'we had so little time together.'"

It looked to Lily like Julian might cry. "Are you okay?" she said. She fought the desire to gather him into her arms.

"I just wish I could stop feeling for a while." Julian said. "I never stop missing him."

Despite a pang of jealousy, Lily reached out and gently stroked Julian's arm. "What are we supposed to do with all of this?"

Julian looked at her tenderly. "I don't know," he said. "I just don't know."

CHAPTER 16

Thou demandest what is love? It is that powerful attraction towards all that we conceive, or fear, or hope beyond ourselves, when we find within our own thoughts the chasm of an insufficient void, and seek to awaken in all things that are, a community with what we experience within ourselves...

—Percy Bysshe Shelley

Julian was combining oak leaf lettuce and baby spinach in a salad bowl when the phone rang.

"Evan, hi! How are you?" Julian said, finally ending the game of phone tag he'd been playing with his friend. He did not like answering machines, and Evan was one of the few people for whom Julian left messages.

"I'm good. How about you? What have you been up to?" Evan said.

"I'm doing okay. I've been painting—nothing too weird—and I'm even teaching art history part-time at a local college."

"I'm glad to hear you're beginning to join the world of the living again, Juls."

"Yeah, well, I suppose I had to venture out of my monastery at some point."

"Speaking of venturing, what's going on with Lily?"

"Actually, I'm in the middle of fixing a salad to bring over to her house for dinner."

Julian anchored the phone between his ear and shoulder, tore off a few more lettuce leaves and tossed them into the bowl. "We've been spending time together, that's all. It's been good for me. It's definitely helped me become less preoccupied with my own misery." Julian took a breath. "How's Marc?"

"He's doing great. I'm telling you, that man is like the eye of a hurricane. All hell can break loose around him, and he remains totally calm."

"Just like you, huh?" Julian teased.

"Me? Right. I take everything too personally, too much to heart." Evan switched back to his original subject. "So what's *really* going on with Lily? You two have been hanging out almost every week for the last two months. I've been concerned."

"Nothing's *going on*. We care about each other and enjoy each other's company. We like the same films, we cook together, and we can talk about art, which is important to both of us. She's like a sister soul."

"Be careful, Julian. From what you've told me, this is a woman who's deeply in love with you. Make sure she's not still hoping for something more than a friendship."

"Thanks for your concern, Evan, but I think I have a handle on the situation." Julian's reply resounded more sharply than he'd meant it to.

Silence. Then—"Well, I know you have to get going," Evan said, with an overly polite edge. "Will you be coming up to the city again any time soon?"

"Probably not until the fall." Julian paused. "I'll call you back when I have more time to talk. I'm fine, Ev. I really am. Send my love to Marc. And anyone else you see."

"I will. Bye Juls. Take care."

"I love you," Julian said.

"I know. Me, too. Bye."

In spite of sounding so certain he was on top of the "situation," Julian wasn't. Yet being around Lily felt good, and he had to admit he enjoyed the adoration. There was an easiness between them that encouraged him to stretch beyond his self-inflicted personal and even artistic limitations. Little by little, he was able to put his love for Sam in a more comfortable, non-emotionally intrusive space, to find a sense of himself and his art that didn't depend on the approval of anyone.

Julian took a peeler out of the drawer and shaved a carrot into wide, curled fronds. He opened a can of artichoke hearts and a container of kalamata olives, drained them and arranged the vegetables on top of the greens.

Was it so wrong to enjoy seeing the best of himself reflected back through the eyes of someone who loved him? Even if he didn't love her in the exact same way? Who's to say how love should be expressed? He covered the salad bowl with a large piece of plastic wrap.

Be careful, Julian. Evan's admonition echoed in his

conscience. He wondered if his loneliness could be causing him to make selfish rationalizations about his relationship with Lily. He knew he could be self-centered at times, but he didn't think he was insensitive to Lily's feelings. He understood they went deep, that she always carried the disappointment of their sexual circumstance. But once his homosexuality was out in the open, he felt he'd been honest about what could not be changed. Loving was an intricate matter when its edge followed a totally unfamiliar shape, yet he didn't think the affinity he felt for Lily was some frivolous "using" of her affections.

Julian glanced at the clock. He was late. He scooped some hazelnut coffee into a container and placed it on top of the salad bowl. Then, gathering everything in the crook of one arm, he grabbed his keys and headed for the door.

"Come on in," Lily called from the kitchen, where she was putting the finishing touches on dinner.

Julian placed the salad on the counter and embraced Lily. "Hi," he said, smiling.

"Hi yourself." They exchanged a kiss. "Your hair smells like juniper."

"Juniper? It must be the new shampoo I used."

"I like it. Besides, juniper is one of my favorite words."

"You have favorite words?" Julian found the thought amusing.

"Sure."

"Like what?"

"Like..." Lily thought for a moment. "Like amethyst.

Shine. Jasmine. Plume. Magnificence. Rounded." She enunciated their richness. "Some words just have pleasing, poetic feel about them. A shape, a texture. Some I like for their melody. Translucent. Cacophony. Perspicacious. Diaphanous."

"I've always liked the word serendipity."

"Good word. Speaking of language, Zhul," Lily deliberately recited his name in French, "I've been having fun with the Magnetic Poetry Kit you gave me. I've been trying to see how many poems I can make without re-using any of the tiles. So far, I've got four. They're kind of strange and I'm not even sure I'd call them poems, but I got hooked on it for a while."

"I'm glad. I haven't touched it since Sam died. He'd used it to leave me what he called, 'kitchen messages.' He loved doing things like that." For a few seconds, Julian hovered in memory, then moved toward the refrigerator. "Can I look at what you've done?"

"Of course."

While Lily spooned dill sauce over the poached salmon she'd prepared, Julian read the first two poems.

> in a diamond moment
> beneath
> the twisted shadow
> of a life unsung
> a whispered symphonys
> recalled
>
> play it easy
> like a summer wind

upon the lazy
fiddle of a day

*   *   *

when winter slips
its smooth white skin
and purple fingers
delirious with light
stroke the peach of spring
time
in gorgeous dress
leaves me panting
trips by tongue
rocks my soaring
breast as I lie newly
graced in green

"I love them, Lily."

"They were fun. I have them on paper. I'll show you the rest later, okay?"

"Sure." Julian took the plastic wrap off the salad he brought and separated the olives, which had all fallen to one side.

"I thought we'd eat on the patio." Lily poured the leftover sauce in a small glass bowl and arranged the dishes on a tray.

"Just what I was thinking." Julian grabbed the salad bowl. "I'll take this out."

He came back in and helped Lily carry the rest of the food and wine to the table. Two places were set across from each other, gardenia blossoms floating in a cobalt blue bowl between them. Julian poured two glasses of zinfandel and passed one to Lily. "This looks fabulous," he said, perusing the salmon and asparagus garnished with lemon slices and diced red peppers. He offered Lily a warm sesame roll from the basket sitting to his right. Over the last two months, they'd spent several such evenings together, and they both settled into its familiar comfort.

Julian raised his glass. "Here's to us."

"To us," Lily echoed, "in the gloaming." They toasted the melting ball of fiery light that was spreading its liquid tangerine across the horizon.

"When I was a kid," Julian said, "I thought the moment the sun set was magical. I believed if I made a wish and repeated it three times, finishing exactly as the last ray dropped out of sight, the wish would come true. I used to stare out of my bedroom window trying to match my last words to the sunset."

"You have to live in the suburbs to be able to do that out of your bedroom window." Lily poured dressing over the salad and tossed it lightly. She put a portion in each of two bowls.

"I forgot. You were a city kid."

"Worse than that. I was a Bronx kid. Remember? At least before we moved to New Rochelle when I was sixteen. I grew up on a street with apartment buildings and no trees. Well, actually, there were once trees bordering the edge of the sidewalks, but when I was about ten, the city dug them all up and covered the soil with large squares of concrete. A little after that, I noticed tufts of grass and one lonely dandelion trying to grow in-between the cracks of cement, fighting hard for life. Maybe that's why I love my flowers so much. I never forgot it. It was so sad, I cried. I really did."

"You poor baby," Julian teased. He lifted a forkful of salmon.

"The only place I could see a sunset was from the vacant lot on the corner," Lily continued, still in her remembering. "I used to go there with my best friend Mindy and collect small pieces of mica that had broken off from larger rocks. I liked to see them glisten in the sunlight. I would wrap the best specimens in tissue and take them home to put into my treasure box." Lily paused. "It seems I'm still drawn to collecting jewels."

"That's what it often feels like I'm doing. Collecting Juls. All the scattered pieces of him."

"You poor baby," Lily mimicked, eating a little too quickly in an effort to catch up to Julian.

"The food is great. Thanks for cooking tonight."

Lily smiled. "I'm glad you like it."

Julian reached for the bottle of zinfandel. "Do you want more wine?"

"No, thanks."

"To another wonderful dinner," he said, lifting his glass.

"I can't tell you how nice it is to eat with a man who enjoys a little variety in his menu. Not that that's your only attraction." Lily tenderly caressed Julian with her eyes.

Julian matched her smile, but his seemed a gesture with a complicated design. Although Lily hadn't intended subtext beneath her words, she felt Julian had read some into them. She hadn't even realized what she'd said until it was too late. The fact she still grieved the loss of him as a lover was something she knew she had to bear. It did no good bringing up the subject. She knew doing so might jeopardize every other wonderful thing they shared.

Lily switched the conversation to a lighter vein. "Nine years of Michael's limited food preferences almost did my taste buds in. I mean, how many Tuesday nights can you eat regular spaghetti and Old World Ragu. Yuck."

"Yuck is right. So how did you get to be such a good cook?"

"Sometimes I'd cook for friends, or just for myself. I'd find a recipe that intrigued me and try it just for the fun of it. Cooking inspires me. I like the way different foods look together, and the way their colors and textures make a kind of edible art."

"Picasso on a plate."

"And you've consumed my entire masterpiece."

"Yum."

When they finished dinner, Julian began to clear the table.

Don't bother, Jul. I'll do it later. It's so lovely out here tonight. Stay and watch the end of the sunset."

"It's perfect, isn't it."

From the patio, they could see a broad expanse of mountains silhouetted in the distance. When only a faint brightness remained, Julian offered to brew coffee for himself, and put the kettle on for Lily. Lily followed him inside. *Baia*, the last song on an old Stan Getz/Charlie Byrd album, *Jazz Samba*, had finished and Lily felt in the mood for Chopin. The haunting melancholy of his music seemed so often to echo her own.

Julian met her out on the patio with the coffee and tea.

"I hope you don't mind a little Chopin," Lily said.

"*Très triste, cherie.*"

Lily loved that Julian spoke to her in French. She'd always been drawn to the language.

"*Oui.* It *is* a little sad, but it's an exquisite sadness," Lily said, as the last singular, sustained notes of the *Waltz in A-Flat* faded, and the *Ballade in G Minor* drifted through the open doorway. "Zhul, did you ever see the movie *Impromptu* about Chopin and George Sand?" Here she was, again thinking about relationships with unhappy circumstances.

"Twice," Julian replied. Once at the theatre and once on video.

"This piece is what George first hears Chopin playing behind closed doors."

"I remember," Julian said. "When she brushes her ear against the door and kind of trances out."

Lily laughed. Julian continually surprised her. "Then," she went on, "George climbs through his window and hides beneath the grand piano listening to him play. When he discovers her, Chopin throws her out, but before she leaves, she says—'I've seen you at last, and I'm delighted to find you're not a man at all. You're an angel. Hands. Halo. Wings. Everything. Good night, my dream.'" Lily recited with exaggerated pathos, but inside, she felt an unembellished truth.

"You've memorized the dialogue?"

"Just a few choice lines," Lily teased. I think Chopin

was the only man George truly loved, that for her, his music represented a spiritual ideal she'd looked for desperately. Also, it's difficult not to fall in love with someone who can create something so moving."

"Just because a person has a great artistic gift, it doesn't make him inherently more worth loving," Julian replied.

"No. But I think we're naturally drawn to things that uplift the spirit, and that when we recognize the humanly divine in a person, we can forgive a lot more of the divinely human."

"There have been too many inspired artists," Julian said, "who were and are less than inspiring human beings."

"I suppose so." Lily sipped her tea, winding out of the conversation and into the silent symphony of fireflies that drew her attention.

Julian joined her audience for a while, then got up from the table and stretched. A lush wave of fragrance floated over from a nearby bush. "The gardenia smells wonderful," he said, as he slipped into Lily's favorite lounge chair.

Lily breathed in the sweet air. "Mind if I sit with you?" She tried to be careful of gestures Julian might interpret as romantic, but that evening she couldn't resist.

"Of course not." Julian beckoned her with his hand.

Lily slid next to him, tucked herself against his chest. He kissed her hair. For several minutes, she closed her eyes, rode the sensations around them—the pulsing roar of cicadas, the piquant waft of yellow star jasmine, the rhythmic fullness of Julian's breathing.

"Have you heard from Evan and Marc?" Lily said. She

felt as if she knew them.

"Actually, Evan called right before I left the house tonight." Julian paused. "He's worried about me."

"How come?"

"Oh, he just wants to make sure I'm taking care of myself."

"So do I."

Julian pressed Lily to him for a moment. "Can I see your other refrigerator poems?" he said.

Lily guessed that was a sign he thought they were getting too physically intimate. "Sure," she said. "I'll get them."

Lily returned with the poems. She brought a candle over and handed them to Julian. "I call the series Magnetic Muse. You've already seen the first two. I was beginning to run out of words when I got to these."

"Read to me. I love to hear you recite your poetry."

"I'm still not used to anyone besides Sara being truly interested in listening to what I've written."

"Read!" Julian said.

And Lily read.

Magnetic Muse 3

together
we could sing the sea
to mist and cool
the crying moon
and think a reigning
vision into sun
one garden

our petals never
bloom apart

Julian thought of Sam, then Lily. He looked at her and smiled. "It's lovely," he said.

Lily read the last poem.

Magnetic Muse 4

from essential places
gray as crushing love
death watches true
he stares
like shadowed sleep
at she who moans
all bare and delicate
an after pictured lover
aching some
but mostly gone

Suddenly, Lily's spontaneously arranged left-over words took on a frightening significance. *An after-pictured lover, aching some, but mostly gone.* Is that, she thought, what I will soon become?

CHAPTER 17

*Your absence has gone through
me like thread through a needle*

—William Stanley Merwin

For Lily, it had been a shining summer, but in the twilight thick of August, a subtle grayness swept over her like a slow cloud eclipsing the sun. Lily had lost herself in Julian, made his life the center of her own. She fell deeply into what she knew was bottomless and dangerous—the hope that something miraculous would change their circumstances. On the surface, she denied that their sexual situation mattered, but the truth found release in other dimensions.

In her dreams, Lily often re-lived the one time she and Julian made love. She awakened with the pain of separation aching in her bones and knots of frustration circling the perimeters of her heart. She tried to loosen them in a long walk, or cover them with Strauss, or drown them in cups of chamomile tea, but nothing helped, and at times she found herself plummeting into a deep, earthly despair.

When she wasn't working, Lily moped around the house, feeling Julian's imprint in every corner. There was nothing now that had remained untouched by his presence. Even the most remote things could be traced to thoughts of him. A blue thumbtack—blue was Julian's favorite color; a postage stamp—she'd saved the Georgia O'Keefe stamp from a card Julian had sent her; anchovies—Julian actually liked anchovies.

It was Saturday and Lily took the day off, her first Saturday off in a while. She hadn't seen Julian since he'd come for dinner over two weeks before, and needed to try to shake herself out of this melancholy mood. She called Sara.

"I've been feeling wretched," she said, "and I need to get over it. Do you want to do something?"

"Sure," Sara replied. "How about we go to lunch and spend some money?"

"I saw a pair of earrings downtown that might cheer me up."

"Good. I'll even drive."

"Can you come about one?" Lily said.

"I'll be there."

Lily and Sara walked out of the fine craft gallery into the mid-day sun. The steady humidity of the previous week had finally lifted, and the air began to hint at the crispness of autumn.

"Do you like them?" Lily said, turning her head from

side to side, testing the weight of her new adornment. The earrings she selected were an original design in etched silver. The top was round with a carved green scarab set in a bezel. A triangular section dropped upside down below it, and from the point hung stacked pieces of spiny oyster shell, coppery jasper and turquoise.

"They're fantastic on you. They bring out the green in your eyes and the auburn highlights in your hair."

"Julian always notices my jewelry. He says his favorite earrings are those dangly silver circles with the bone and lapis beads I often wear. He likes the way they move and jingle and catch the light."

Sara smiled. "Are you hungry?"

"Not really," Lily said. "Breakfast sort of turned into brunch, so I ate not too long before we left. How about you?"

"I'm not that hungry either. How about we get something hot to drink and maybe a pastry?" Sara always seized the opportunity for an afternoon sweet.

"That sounds good."

Arm in arm, Lily and Sara walked down the tree-lined street, past a Japanese restaurant, a new art gallery, an imported clothing store, and toward one of their favorite outdoor cafés. They found a relatively shady table under the awning that hung above the front windows.

"I'll go in and order," Sara said. "Do you want peppermint tea?"

"Yes. And two hazelnut biscotti. Thanks."

Alone for the moment, Lily's mind again seized upon Julian. She recalled how she had sat with him at that same table, under a round yellow moon. They'd sipped wine, talked about art and emptiness, the taste of crème brulée, the shape of stars. If only he would stay out of my dreams, she thought. The memory of what it felt like to slide her hand along the smoothness of his back, or press her lips against the hollow of his neck made her ache for him. *How much longer can I pretend?* She had almost let that thought come into full consciousness when Sara returned with the drinks and desserts.

"What did you get?" Lily asked, helping Sara arrange the table.

"A latté, and raspberry chocolate mousse cake."

"Looks good."

Sara sliced off a forkful and let it dissolve on her tongue. "This is absolutely orgasmic!" she said. "Do you want a taste?"

"No thanks." Sex was the last thing Lily wanted to think about. "I'll stick with my biscotti."

Lily poured hot water over the tea bag in her cup. "Something's shifting with Julian," she said. "I can feel it."

"What do you mean?"

"I don't know. He doesn't call as often as he used to. He says he's been busy with his own stuff. Yet, the last time we were together, he seemed his usual warm, engaging self."

"When was that?"

"Eighteen days ago."

"Eighteen, huh."

"So I've been counting. So what?"

Sara held her hands up in surrender. "So nothing," she said.

"He came over for dinner. We watched the sunset.

Those times with him are so incredible."

Lily pushed from her mind the thought that the "shift" she was sensing might have to do with Julian feeling her tug on him and becoming frightened by it. She could barely look at the possibility that, as much as he cared for her, he never lost sight of the fact that the two of them were bound to come to a place where, for certain purposes, their paths must fork. A place where the tangled mire of their circumstance would prevent them from together going any further.

"Lily, can I say something you may not want to hear?"

Lily hesitated. "What?"

"This is not a mutually romantic relationship you're in. You can't think of Julian as someone with whom you might have an intimate future. You've got to come to terms with the fact that that's not what this is about."

Lily kept silent. She twirled her index finger through a tuft of hair. If she actually spoke out loud any words that would agree with what Sara was saying, her precariously constructed semi-denial would begin to crumble, and she wasn't ready to see it fall. Instead, she kept it carefully anchored to the corners of her mind, putting as much distance as she could between it and anything that might begin to shake it loose.

"Are you okay?" Sara asked.

"Yes. But I don't want to go there."

"Do it now or do it later," Sara replied, "but someday you're going to have to stop cruising down that ancient river in Egypt."

Lily changed the subject. "So how's the novel coming?"

"It seems to be writing itself pretty effortlessly right now. I finished the love scene in the apple orchard, and I've got Old Reba mixing her green and yellow teas, asking those who might never understand the question, 'When are you going to liberate your heart?'"

Whether purposely or not, Lily knew Sara had wound back onto the subject of denial.

"And just what does it mean to liberate one's heart?" Lily said.

"When Old Reba says it, it means to stop playing mind tricks with yourself and begin to look closely at the face of your own shadow."

"When did you get so wise, Sara of the 'one-more-cigarette-won't-hurt-me-they-make-too-much-of-lung-cancer' attitude?" Lily teased.

But Sara wasn't laughing. "When a good friend helped me see the flaw in my thinking and I stopped kidding myself."

"I'm sorry. I know it took a lot of courage for you to quit smoking."

"It also takes courage to turn from an emotional addiction."

"An emotional addiction? Is that what you think my relationship with Julian is?"

"Are you saying it's not?"

Lily squirmed in the horror of that thought.

Sara continued. "Don't try to fool yourself into thinking it's any less destructive than a physical or psychological addiction."

Lily let down her defenses. "I cannot not love him, Sara."

"You know you don't have to stop loving him, but you do have to stop hopelessly wishing for something that will never change. End of lecture."

"I hear you, Sara. I'm just not talking back."

When Lily got home she felt physically and emotionally exhausted. She headed for the bedroom and carefully removing her new earrings, she placed them in the rosewood jewelry box that sat on the bureau. "Maybe Julian's pulling away is just my imagination," she said aloud to the weary face in the mirror. Her solar plexus tightened in response to her self-deceit. She thoughtlessly ran her nails over her left palm.

Lily slipped out of her skirt and fell onto the bed. Fighting the truth was exhausting. So now Sara thinks I'm hooked on Julian like he's some kind of emotional intoxicant, she thought. She could feel a rumble of anger begin in her belly. She doesn't understand. "I am *not addicted* to Julian," she said aloud, repeating the words like a mantra. "I am not addicted to Julian. I am not. I am not! I am..." Lily's sandcastle of denial disintegrated into a sea of tears. "I can't stop wanting him." She couldn't bear to think she would never again hold or kiss or touch this man she so dearly loved. And like Heloise, she couldn't bear *not* to think it. Sara's right, she thought. Every cell of me is drunk with him.

You've come back to do it differently this time. Lovina's words resounded in Lily's mind with a clarity that startled her. What is this, a psychic free for all? she mentally shouted. *Just a reminder*, the voice said. Lily felt she had become pathetic. She was disgusted with her own melodramatics and self-pity. They were an embarrassment, and they weren't doing her or Julian any good. She knew she didn't have to stop loving him, but she did have to stop grieving what might have been, what could never be. It was time. For Heloise and for her.

Lily got up and went into the bathroom. She turned on the bathtub tap and added a calming herbal mixture to the rushing water. She would try to cleanse herself of the anguish that had lived within her far too long. She would immerse herself in a wash of fragrant, healing warmth and let the torment of lifetimes float away. When the tub was full, Lily reached for her bath sponge and got in. "I thought I was doing so well," she whispered. She cringed at how she'd fooled herself into believing she was beyond hoping for miracles. Lifting the soaking sponge, Lily slid it slowly along her arm. Rivulets of water separated, rolling off to each side. She wondered if Julian, too, was sliding away.

CHAPTER 18

*The need to become a separate self is as
urgent as the yearning to merge forever.*

—Judith Viorst

Julian was putting the finishing touches on a painting
he'd been working on, trying not to think about what he'd
done the night before. How he'd had sex with Thomas, a
man he'd only recently met and didn't even know if he
liked. How, afterwards, he felt he'd somehow been
unfaithful to Sam...*and* to Lily, who he'd been avoiding
for weeks. He took a final look at his canvas. Satisfied, he
put the caps back on several tubes of paint. Over the
months his art had come a long way. His New York work
had glared all edges and angles, defined geometry, and
Julian now thought it...untrue. He remembered the
control with which he'd executed the placement of each
line, each stroke, how he'd squelched the blurry-edged
galaxy of emotion that spiraled within him threatening to
explode. Its intensity had frightened him. If he'd given it

free rein, his work might have appeared capricious, artistically undisciplined. What would Sam have thought?

Julian considered those first weeks in Asheville painting nothing but a tortured monk, a half-built cathedral, ancient inner and outer landscapes, just a weird creative fluke. Although he'd saved the canvases, he couldn't bear to look at them. He'd stacked them against an out-of-the-way wall and thought he was again finished with painting. But things had changed when Sam cajoled him back to the easel.

It had happened on one of his sleepless nights, shortly after the embarrassing intimate interlude with Lily. After tossing for a while under the covers, Julian sat up in bed staring into the dark. Suddenly he heard a voice. *It's time*, it whispered. He was certain it was Sam. Even though Julian often talked to him to ease the loneliness, Sam had never talked back. Yet, instead of fear, Julian felt calmed and comforted by his lover's ghostly presence. *It's time.* The words echoed in Julian's mind. Sound floated back to him from every corner. *It's time...time...time.*

Julian knew what Sam's message meant, and that sense of creative urgency overtook him. In a strange way, he also knew the sudden inspiration was connected to Lily. The pain and confusion around what had happened between them whirled inside him, pushing for an artistic outlet, a way to make some sense out of his feelings. Even after decades of painting, Julian felt he hadn't produced anything worthwhile. He wasn't even sure he was capable of it. Deep inside, he'd often felt his work was marked by nothing more than triviality, that it made a mockery of art.

Cautiously, he dragged himself out of bed. The last

time he'd had that kind of inspiration terrible things manifested. But this felt different. This was Sam cajoling him. Julian set a canvas on his easel and squeezed out several depressing colors. He'd grown used to painting with them. He'd hardly finished the first few brushstrokes when again he heard the voice. *Life*, Sam said, in a familiar tone he'd used when he'd become a little exasperated with Julian. "Okay," Julian whispered. He added to his pallet cerulean, emerald, violet, fuchsia, gamboge—the colors of sky and sea and summer meadow, of wildflowers and sunrise. Shapes began to form, none with sharp edges. Julian worked intently. He liked what he saw happening in front of him. It was filled with vitality and promise. Sam, too, seemed pleased. *Now you're on to something, Juls.*

Even though Sam returned to silence, Julian continued to paint. And his work *did* take on new life. He seemed finished with the colors of a disturbing past and it felt good to be painting things that uplifted him. Now he cleaned his brushes, tidied up around the studio and jumped into the shower. He soaped a washcloth and circled it over his chest and arms, down his torso, over his genitals. Why should he feel guilty about last night? As much as he would always love Sam, Sam was gone. And it had been a very long time since he'd been touched in an intimate way...by a man. Julian admitted that part of the reason he'd slept with Thomas was to reassure himself of his homosexuality. Now, in that arena at least, he felt satisfied nothing had changed.

Julian poured shampoo into the palm of his hand and lathered his hair. It smelled of juniper and he thought of Lily. He hadn't seen her since dinner at her house almost three weeks before. *Lily.* What would she think if she knew of his impulsive sexual encounter? But there was no reason for him to tell her. That part of his life was separate from their relationship. And what exactly their relationship at that point was troubled Julian. Often, Lily acted as if they were a couple, in a romantic sense. He knew it must be difficult for her, but Lily's unreal expectations, even if she denied them, were evident and difficult for Julian. Though he loved her in the best way he could, he wasn't sure anymore how to be around her. Lately, there seemed to be a subtext to their interaction based on Lily's hope for the impossible.

Julian rinsed off, dried himself and took a personal inventory. He needed a haircut. And at almost forty, he wasn't young anymore. If he didn't start working out again, his previously cared-for body would turn to flab. Since Sam's death, he'd hardly gone to the gym, and except for the occasional hike with Lily, he'd become lazy. He was already showing too much gut. Although last night there were no complaints. Julian half-smiled at the thought, the way someone might who enjoyed the secret of a defiant act more than the act itself. Years ago, before Sam, he wouldn't have given a second thought to a casual sexual indulgence. But now that he'd learned to open his heart, nothing felt casual, and intimate indulgences carried emotional consequences.

Julian slipped on jeans and a T-shirt and headed for the kitchen. It was already mid-afternoon and he hadn't eaten anything since breakfast. He found some cold left over chicken and green beans. Starved, he didn't bother to sit down. He stood at the counter, picking with his fingers.

Lately, Julian had been making excuses not to see Lily. It wasn't that he didn't want to be with her, but that he was becoming frightened of hurting her. He could never be what she wanted him to be, and giving her more opportunity to hope seemed unfair. She deserved better.

After his conversation with Lily at the Botanical Gardens, Julian had thought much about the seeming synchronicity that had brought them together. He didn't know whether or not he really believed he and Lily *were* Abelard and Heloise in a reincarnational sense, although he'd been curious enough to buy a copy of *The Letters of Heloise and Abelard,* the first four of which he'd read, the personal ones. They disturbed him, yet he found himself trying to understand Abelard's perspective, at times allowing himself to identify with it. He hadn't told Lily. If she knew he'd read the letters, it might give her one more thing that united them, one more thing to grasp onto. He wasn't sure that was best for either of them. Besides, the subject rarely came up anymore. There seemed to be an unspoken understanding between them to keep the focus in the present.

Julian knew he needed to see Lily, to talk with her about their relationship, where it was, and where it would never go. This was as much for her as for him. After too many "sorry I can't make it" or "I'm really busy" excuses, Lily probably wondered why he didn't want to be with her. Although Julian thought their relationship needed to switch directions, he didn't feel it was over.

Julian dialed Lily's number. After four rings, the answering machine picked up. For Lily, Julian bent his I-don't-talk-to-machines rule.

"Sorry I haven't called lately," he said. He felt uneasy. "If you're free tomorrow, I'd like to come over in the afternoon. We can hang out or watch a video." He paused. "Okay...well...let me know. Bye."

Julian hung up. He knew Lily would detect in his voice that something was different. He wondered how in the world he could say to her what needed to be said and not break her heart.

CHAPTER 19

Once I falsely hoped to meet with beings, who,
pardoning my outward form, would love me for the
excellent qualities I was capable of bringing forth...

—Mary Shelley
Frankenstein

"It's the Frankenstein story yet again," Lily said, as she pressed the rewind button on the VCR remote. She and Julian had spent their Sunday afternoon watching *Powder*. "It's the world's inability to embrace what it doesn't understand, that which is phenomenal and even miraculous."

"Yeah, it is." Julian reached for another handful of popcorn. He'd been channeling tension into eating.

"It's the failure to recognize worth when it doesn't come in a socially acceptable package." Lily slid the popcorn bowl to Julian's side of the coffee table. "Appearance in this world is everything," she continued, knowing Julian understood. "And anyone who doesn't fit into accepted parameters is feared. His spirit is broken, he's driven to desperate acts, and the world ultimately feels justified in destroying him. It's the incredible loneliness of being different."

"*There's* a truth close to my own heart," Julian said softly.

Lily knew he was referring to being gay, but she had the loneliness of a different situation in mind.

"It's also *Moby Dick*," Julian said. They were on a roll. "The quote Powder recites is from Melville—'*Where lies the final harbor where we unmoor no more...*'"

"Are you sure?"

"I know my Melville. He was gay, you know," Julian teased. "Anyway, Powder is an albino, like Moby, both of them thought of as aberrations. But they both also possess something grand, even threatening, and people wind up projecting onto them the fear of their own inadequacies."

"Or maybe the fear of their own magnificence," Lily said.

"I hadn't thought of that."

"Somewhere," Julian said, "Melville says it was as if Ahab piled upon Moby Dick the sum of all the rage and hate of his entire race from Adam down. Maybe Ahab thought the only way he could make himself equal to his self-appointed nemesis was to destroy him. His obsession came from his own sense of smallness. In the end, what's motivated by fear and revenge can't triumph."

"You remember a lot more about Moby Dick than I'd ever want to." Lily scooped a handful of popcorn from the bowl.

"Evan and I have had some of this discussion before."

"It was not one of my favorite books." Lily recalled the difficulty of trying to read things she didn't resonate with or had little interest in, even if they were considered brilliant. "To me," she said, "the most pathetic creature is still the Frankenstein monster. No one can embrace or befriend Mary Shelley's monster, not even his creator. There's a terrible consequence for withholding love."

"And for not taking responsibility for what you create," Julian said. "Frankenstein can't do it, and Powder's father denies his son over and over."

"It's so sad."

Julian hovered in a similar memory. "My own father disowned me for two years when he found out I was gay."

"You never told me."

"I was in my twenties at the time. He wouldn't speak a word to me, wouldn't eat at the same table when I visited, would walk right by me on the street as if I didn't exist."

"Julian, how awful."

"It was. It isn't that way now, but I'm still not completely comfortable around him."

Lily rose from the rocker where she'd been curled and moved next to Julian on the couch. She took his hand in hers and brought it to her lips. After a minute, Julian gently freed himself.

"Lily," he whispered. He stood up and began to slowly pace the room. "I think we need to talk. About us."

Lily could feel every cell of her stiffen in anticipation of what was coming. "What about us?" The strength she'd been determined to hold onto since she'd answered Julian's phone message the night before had fractured.

Julian hesitated for a moment. "I think it would be best if we didn't spend so much time together."

"Best for whom?" Lily said, more loudly than she'd intended. Without warning, the words of an ancient but familiar drama slipped from her throat. "Are you presuming to know what's best for me? Again?" Heloise hovered beneath her words. "You can't get rid of me so easily this time. Banishing a woman to a convent is no longer so convenient."

Julian stopped pacing. "I read the letters, Lily."

Lily's eyes darted toward him.

"I think, under the circumstances, Abelard did the best he knew to do."

"And what was that?" Lily could feel an ancient anger rising. Her voice grew agitated. "To send Heloise to a convent and then to abandon her for years? To claim that everything they'd shared, everything she held beautiful and sacred had been lustful, vile and unholy? That was the best he knew to do?" Lily stared at Julian waiting for a response.

"No, but…" Julian paused too long.

Lily interrupted. "Maybe he never even loved her. If he had, how could he have come to think of their passion as sinful and repulsive? Maybe you think of me as repulsive?" She hadn't realized she carried those feelings until they tumbled from her lips.

"No. No, Lily."

Julian walked back to the couch, removed a throw pillow and slid next to Lily. He reached for her arm. She pulled away, backing herself into a corner. She raised her knees to her chest, arms around them.

"I've never been repulsed by you...or by any woman," Julian said. "I'm just not drawn to women in a sexual way. Like Heloise, you've taken the situation as a personal outrage against you."

"I'm sorry, Julian, but to me the *situation* sometimes feels a lot like rejection."

"Well it's not. It's not at all about rejection. I don't think Abelard intentionally meant to hurt Heloise, and I'm not meaning to hurt you. This is not some kind of punishment, Lily. My sexual preference is not your punishment. It would be punishing both of us if we continued to deny the limitations of our relationship. We might wind up like Carrington and Strachey—you *do* know about them—tortured by the loneliness of an incomplete love. She dissolved herself so into him that when he died, she ended up blasting a shotgun through her heart."

Lily turned sharply toward Julian. "Don't be so dramatic."

"*I'm* not the drama queen here."

In spite of herself, Lily had to smile at the truth of his observation.

Julian moved closer to her and continued gently. "I can feel you subtly pulling on me, wanting something I can't give you. And I sense an anger in you at times, as if you think the cosmos has deliberately dealt you a losing hand—the 'old perpetual complaint against God,' Abelard called it. My sexual identity is not an act of treachery against you by some vengeful deity."

"You're as much attached to your gayness as Abelard was to his castration. You look at everything in your life from that perspective, not from the perspective of the heart alone."

"You're wrong, Lily." Julian stood up, walked a few steps away. "I don't think I do, but..." He turned to her. Curled up tightly, now hugging a pillow, she looked fragile and beautiful and Julian hated what he was going to say. "Can you honestly tell me you could be happy in a relationship with no sexual intimacy?"

Lily didn't answer. She was through lying.

"Especially," Julian continued, "with someone you know you're drawn to loving in that way? In this arena, perhaps it *is* more difficult for you."

A rush of empty, endless space opened inside of Lily. She bolted toward Julian, folded herself against his chest. "I don't want to lose you."

Julian took Lily's face in his hands. "We don't have to lose each other." He kissed her softly. "We have to find our selves." Julian led her back to the couch. "Sit next to me," he said. "I'm not abandoning you. I can't imagine my life without you in it, but I think we have to be honest about what we both need and realistic about how much of it we can have with each other."

Lily felt defeated, but knew Julian was right. "I know. I know I've held too tightly and hoped too hard. I've tried to hide it from myself, but I've known we would come to this point. Even Lovina saw it. I didn't want to tell you."

"What did she say?"

"She saw other partners for each of us, people with whom we would be able to have a meaningful yet emotionally manageable relationship? She said that on a scale of intensity from one to ten, we were about a seventeen."

Julian laughed. "She sure got that right. And if there are to be other relationships, we don't have to think about that now." He put his arm around Lily, drew her close.

"No. But..." Lily was ready to own that what was happening was inevitable. "I guess we do have to decide about us, about how to go forward from here."

"All I'm suggesting," Julian said, "is that we face the truth of our situation, leave ourselves open to other social opportunities. It doesn't mean we won't still see each other and do things together, but maybe we need to become more independent. Maybe we've both held on too tightly."

"I love you, Julian. I can't help it. I adore you." Lily did not say this in the hopes of changing or manipulating anything. It was merely the truth that spilled from her heart, and Julian understood it in just that way.

"I know," Julian said. "I love you, too. Very much. You came into my life at a time when I was confused and frightened and terribly lonely. In a way I could never have anticipated, you gave me the courage to feel again. I will always love you, Lily. Please know that."

Lily and Julian held each other in silence gazing through the window glass at the diminishing brilliance of a sinking sun. The illusion of an ending. Only a perception. Not a truth at all.

CHAPTER 20

A cosmic loneliness was my shadow.

—Zora Neale Hurston

The room was decorated with an eclectic assortment of people, all there to celebrate Maya's twenty-fourth birthday. Outwardly unlikely duets and trios greeted each other with the inner melody of old friends. This was Lily's first leap of social separation from Julian who'd been her almost constant companion most of the summer. She'd seen him only once since the start of their new understanding two weeks before. It seemed to her like ten.

Lily wound across the room toward her hostess, collecting shards of conversation along the way.

"...yeah, I know. Mercury must be retrograde..."

"...you, like, go through this doorway and get sucked into the body of John Malkovich..."

"...*Half Asleep In Frog Pajamas*. I'll lend you the book if you prom..."

"Happy birthday Maya!" Lily handed her a small box

wrapped in magenta foil. Inside, there was a pair of amethyst and gold earrings.

Maya embraced Lily. "Thanks," she said. An unlikely duet stood next to them. "Do you know each other?"

"No," Lily replied.

"Lily, this is Frederick." Maya motioned toward the balding, full-faced man wearing polyester slacks and horn-rimmed glasses. He looked to be in his early sixties. "And this is Moon Blossom," she added, turning toward a thirty-five-ish female representative of the more cosmic population in attendance. The woman, dressed in an ankle-length skirt of many colors topped by deep purple, wore enough quartz crystal around her neck and the six holes in her ears to receive transmissions from the Pleiades. After making the introductions, Maya excused herself and headed for the kitchen.

"So, Lily, what do you do?" Frederick asked.

A ridiculous question, Lily thought. If Frederick had been a little more original, perhaps she wouldn't have felt compelled to toy with him.

"Nothing," she said piously. "I'm a Buddhist."

"Ahhh," Frederick sighed, as if uncertain as to whether or not he'd just been mocked.

Lily turned to the woman who dared to name herself after a celestial body. "So, Moon, what do *you* do?"

Five minutes of conversation with Frederick and Moon Blossom had Lily mapping out the room for her next direction. She spotted Lovina, who had just arrived, heading for the food. Lily made her way over. Lovina was already balancing an indulgent plate of blue corn chips, salsa and guacamole when they greeted each other.

"Lovina, hi!" Lily helped herself to a few carrot and celery sticks and some bean dip. She followed Lovina to a couple of nearby chairs.

"You know eating is one of the two greatest joys of being in a body. Making love being the other. How are you, my dear?"

"Actually, not great. Since I can't make love with the only one I want, I've lost my appetite." Lily put the carrot she'd barely tasted back on her plate.

"Things change. That's the one thing you can always count on."

The other thing you can always count on, Lily thought, was a platitude from Lovina.

"Talk to me, my dear. What's going on with your man?"

"Julian and I have...let's say, faced a little reality. I love him dearly, and I do know he loves me. Even though I tried to deny it, I always knew our relationship could only go so far. Yet I can't help feeling sad that we weren't able to be together in the way I wanted."

"Love is not about what one wants, you know. And it's not even always about being together."

"Great," Lily said, with more than a hint of sarcasm aimed in a general cosmic direction. "So what exactly is it about?"

"You want my love lecture?" Lovina was still happily partaking in the one of her two greatest physical pleasures she could enjoy in public.

"Why not."

"Okay. Here's the short version. Love is not something we can get from another. It isn't something we can fall in or out of, or something we receive in return for anything. Love isn't even some *thing*. Love can't be bought or sold or traded for. It isn't measured by what physical face we happen to be wearing in any given lifetime or how much our body conforms to what is currently in vogue. Love isn't romance, nor is it a reward for deodorized armpits or sweet smelling breath. And, believe it or not, love has little to do with finding a soulmate in order to complete us in some way so that we can then be *in* love— although that kind of intense mirror can greatly accelerate our understanding of what love is.

"Love is that energy, that creative force, that divine alignment we've forgotten we are. It's gardenia in bloom, the miracle of breath, the subtle dazzle of a leaf's uncurl. It's what keeps the stars from spilling into the sea, and the sea from dripping over the edge of infinity. Love is the grace that celebrates the fullest expression of all things, yet knows its true source is in emptiness."

Lily felt Lovina's eyes penetrate her own, and she allowed the words to stand like beacons in the shadows of her loneliness. From the entranced state in which she listened, she saw, for a fleeting moment, the flash of truth.

"Lovina! Am I interrupting?"

Pulled back to the room by the voice of the man who was now standing in front of her, Lily's momentary ray of clarity began to cloud with earthly static, like being startled awake from a profound dream.

"David, hello!" Lovina said. She rose from her chair and embraced her friend.

"I haven't seen you in ages," David said. "How are you?"

"Just hunky dory." Lovina popped the last corn chip into her mouth. "David, this is Lily. And if you two will excuse me for a moment, I'm going to sample some more goodies." She turned toward Lily and flashed a curiously exaggerated smile.

Lily wondered why people were introducing her to other people, then disappearing.

"Lovina is a treasure," David said, taking the now empty chair next to Lily. "She's rescued me more than once from my own pitiful devices."

"I know what you mean," Lily said.

David smiled. "You own InWord Bound, don't you?"

"Yes. I do."

"Maya often talks about how much she enjoys working there. And she speaks so highly of you." David paused. "You know, Lily, I'll admit I was hoping you'd be here tonight. I've wanted to meet you.

"Really." Lily weighed David's words in her mind.

"Yes. Really." He cleared his throat. "So Maya tells me you're a writer."

"I write a little. Mostly poetry these days. How about you? Any Muses hovering around?"

"When I was younger, I played in a band."

"What did you play?" She tried to be polite.

"Guitar."

Despite herself, Lily became curious. There was something about a man who made music. "What kind of music?"

"All kinds. A little folk, a little bluegrass, a little rock and roll, but I really enjoy a good blues jam, especially the old timey stuff like Robert Johnson, Blind Lemon

Jefferson, Muddy Waters."

"How come you gave it up?"

"These days, I'm mostly a therapist."

Lily gathered impressions of David. She caught herself comparing him to Julian and stopped. She did not want to be small-minded. David seemed reasonable enough— intelligent, interesting, amiable. She ran her eye casually over him. He looked almost ten years older than she, maybe in his early fifties, medium tall with a slight thickness above his waist. His light brown hair appeared to be thinning at the crown. His eyes were dark and intense, and he had a neatly trimmed beard which, unlike his hair, was streaked with silver. He wore crisp jeans and a white, collarless cotton shirt with rolled up sleeves.

"How do you know Maya, David?"

"She comes to a meditation group I host."

"Yes. It seems she's mentioned it to me."

"Why don't you join us some time?" David said.

"At this point, writing is my meditation. But I'll keep it in mind."

David changed the subject. "Would you consider having dinner with me some evening?"

Lily had already decided that David might be a little too old for her, and not quite her "type." Besides, she'd never been attracted to men with beards. What might they be hiding? She liked to be able to see a man's face. "Thank you for the invitation," Lily said, "but I've got unresolved emotional business right now that would get in the way of any new friendship. I'm sorry."

"Me, too." David's eyes seemed filled with disappointment. "But I appreciate your honesty," he added, taking a card from his wallet. "Here's my number. Will you call me if you're ever interested in getting together? No promises required. No pressure."

Lily accepted the card with no response other than a smile. Even though she did not feel David was a candidate for her affections, she wondered if she would ever again be drawn to any man.

Lily saw Maya motion David to join her.

"If you'll excuse me," he said, "I'm going to go talk to the birthday girl."

As Lily watched David navigate the crowded room, Lovina ambled over, a paper plate filled to the edges with an assortment of desserts. She gazed at Lily for a moment as if reading her mind. "Forget appearances," she said.

CHAPTER 21

No, my sweet darling, [this is] not the last hand-clasp of the lover who is quitting you, [it is] the embrace of the brother who remains to you. This feeling is too beautiful, too pure and too sweet for me ever to want to have done with it...

—George Sand
to Alfred du Musset

"Before we end our discussion of impressionism," Julian said, addressing his art history class, "I have a theory I'd like to share with you." He stepped away from the edge of the desk where he'd been leaning. "And it's a purely intuitive one, so don't go quoting this as gospel. My theory is that impressionist painting seems to me to be more aligned with what has been called pure consciousness or divine mind than other forms, and expresses this in its essentially nebulous quality."

Because of the unusual circumstances that brought

him and Lily together over the last two seasons, Julian found himself entertaining ideas and using language he would not have considered in the past. And with this expansion of mind came an inner expansion that demanded an honesty and personal integrity with which he was finally becoming comfortable.

"Through impressionist art, it's as if we get to experience the essence of a scene or object in a more interdimensional way, to experience it before it has solidified into physicality with the precisely defined lines and edges and angles we find, for example, in the more grounded cubist work. We get to experience it more purely as light, as mystery, as closer to what some have called the formlessness from which all things take form. It reminds us of our grander selves, of the largest collective potential that exists in all of us.

"In music, this airiness versus solidity feels like Mozart as opposed to Stravinsky. In dance, like Makarova in contrast to Martha Graham—equal in the power to move us, but different in the *way* it moves us. These are my personal feelings and observations, just something to think about. You can accept them or reject them as you wish." Julian looked at the clock. "We can have discussion on this next time if you want. Enjoy your weekend." He gathered his papers and slipped them into an art portfolio that served as his briefcase. Not in the mood for after-class conversation, Julian left quickly. He had things on his mind.

Julian had begun to feel a restlessness that was quickened by the paring down of autumn and the inevitable approach of winter—another winter without the intimate warmth of Sam. He suspected his purpose with Lily had come to an end, felt it was time to leave even the North Carolina mountains that had nurtured and protected him these last months. He had the sense of something else he needed to make a space for, some new outer and inner landscape waiting to be traversed.

He and Sam had dreamed of living in Hawaii, and several weeks before, Julian had been given an opportunity to follow that dream. Turning the possibility over and over in his mind he'd become dizzy with its implications. Finally, he came to a decision. Now, the hardest part seemed to be how to tell Lily. How to help her understand—to help himself understand—this was not good-bye, but *aloha*—love.

That evening, Julian was meeting Lily for dinner on the Sunset Terrace at The Grove Park Inn. Perhaps, he thought, it would be easier to talk about the six thousand miles soon to be between them if they could witness how close the sun, round and gold upon its imaginary descent into night, could feel.

Formed out of boulders of granite excavated from Sunset Mountain, The Grove Park Inn was built in twelve months of 1912-13 without architectural blueprints. The main inn—its original structure—had two six-foot high fireplaces, poetry carved into its stone, and the ghost of a young woman said to have fallen over the fifth floor railing that wrapped around its Palm Court. The Sunset Terrace was situated off the main inn along one whole side of the Great Hall. It felt, to Julian, like being in the safe shadow of a great cave—a good place to begin and end things.

The sky had just become the first purple phase of sunset when he and Lily received their entrées. Lily had hardly found time for a decent lunch and heartily indulged in her pan seared trout. Julian, however, only picked at his filet mignon, pushing slices around his plate, leaving spaces, as he did all evening in their conversation.

"You seem lethargic tonight," Lily said.

"I'm fine." Julian's tone clearly indicated he wasn't."

"How's your class going, Jul?"

"Pretty well. I've enjoyed it," he added, with a private edge of sadness. "So how was Maya's party?"

Lily was eating too quickly. She slowed down. "That was three weeks ago, Julian."

"It was? I don't think I ever asked you about it. Did Sara go with you?"

Lily knew there was something Julian was not saying. "Sara was invited, but had other plans," she replied. "It was an interesting evening. Maya's friends are a diverse group."

"I meant to tell you," Julian said, "I love those earrings." She was wearing the ones with the green scarabs.

"I know. You've told me before." This is ridiculous, Lily thought, as she watched him etch figure-eights into his baked potato. "Julian, my love, are we going to play trivia all evening, or are you going to tell me what's going on? We've come a long way together. I can hear whatever it is you have to say."

Lily and Julian had done well in their commitment to accept one another without expectation, to give each other the freedom to pursue what was important but separate from their relationship. They'd embraced the gift of all that had happened between them, and stopped grieving what had not.

"I'm leaving Asheville," Julian said. He waited to see how Lily was taking the news before he continued. Her eyes shimmered, but she seemed only to be listening. "I have an opportunity to go to Hawaii and paint. It's been a dream of mine—and Sam's—and even though he's not here, Sam has helped to make it possible. It's his cousin, Katherine, who offered me her house with a studio on Kauai. I'm feeling this could lead to a new direction in my art." Julian paused as a sweep of emotion glazed his own eyes.

Lily felt a tear roll down her cheek. She brushed it away. "Even if it doesn't look like it, Jul, I'm happy for you. I really am."

Yet the idea of Julian being so far away tugged at every sinew. *I don't want to forget you. I don't want you to fade like a fraying mental photo until all that's left is the ghost of a smile, a flash of blue, the empty echo of a touch.*

Lily nibbled at her food, while Julian pushed his half-full plate to the side. An orange dome of sun blazed on the horizon.

"I'll miss you," Julian said. "I'll call, of course. And we can write to each other. Maybe you can even come for a visit."

"I would like that," Lily said. But she feared things would change with so much distance. What was once made flesh she knew could become thin as the fabric of a wish, wispy as a filament of long forgotten hope. "When do you think you'll be going?" she asked.

"I've already given notice at the college, and I know someone who wants to take over the lease on my house, so I'll be able to leave in about two weeks."

Julian's words whipped like a cold wind at Lily's heart. "So soon," she whispered.

When she got home, Lily attempted to digest Julian's news, but it sat, unassimilated in her gut with the rest of her dinner. She went to the kitchen cupboard, popped a few Tums, and put the kettle on. Her entire relationship with Julian had been like watching for water to boil, anticipating something that seemed as if it would never happen. But Lily knew she had, in truth, moved beyond those feelings, and that now, in a desperate moment, it was only the ghosts of their twisted façades that appeared.

She really was happy for Julian. Of that Lily was certain. Her heart was able to stretch enough to want for Julian whatever he wished most for himself. But her mind, in its contracted state, felt betrayed by her magnanimity. I have got to get over this, she thought. I have got to let go of these feelings of abandonment, rejection and betrayal. They are not real. They are not even always mine. They have no truth between me and Julian. Oh God, please help me to know this in the only way that matters.

When he got home, Julian plopped himself into an arm chair, not even turning on a light. He, too, felt the shadows of his fear take form around him. How could simply seeing Lily shake the former certainty of his decision? He would miss her, of that he had no doubt. She had been his true friend, confidante, and lover in the largest sense of the word. But now he must go on with his own purpose, his own self-discovery, wherever it might lead him. So why did he feel as if he were committing the ultimate act of betrayal? This is not me, he thought. These are not my feelings. They are not real. They have no truth between me and Lily. Oh God, please help me to know this in the only way that matters.

CHAPTER 22

*You have lifted my very soul up into the light
of your soul, and I am not ever likely to mistake
it for the common daylight.*

—Elizabeth Barrett
to Robert Browning

It was a perfect afternoon for an autumn hike, and one of the last days Lily would get to spend with Julian before he left for Hawaii. The sun shone bright and warm, keeping the chill off the steady breeze. Islands of clouds meandered across a deep cerulean sky. After a picnic of cold chicken and homemade coleslaw, Lily and Julian started out on one of their favorite trails. It was a Monday, weeks before peak leaf season, and they encountered few other hikers.

Now nearing the summit, the trail grew steep and they stopped to stretch and get their breath. The forest reverberated with the chatter and trill of birds, the wild buzz of insects, the rustle of small critters beneath mounds of dried leaves.

"You doing all right?" Julian said.

Lily knew he was asking about more than her physical condition. She smiled. "Yes, I'm fine."

Although she'd tried not to think about Julian's leaving, her mind kept returning to just that. It was the same with Julian, yet neither of them spoke of it. They'd already confessed all their feelings, cried all their tears.

"We're almost there." Julian retied a shoelace that had come undone.

"Yes. Almost."

Sliding her knapsack over her shoulder, Lily continued up the wide railroad-tie steps. Julian followed.

The trail ended and they climbed to a platform surrounded by a low stone wall. A sign warned not to venture beyond. As they had done before, Lily and Julian ignored it. Carefully, they edged over the wall where a large, flat outcropping of rock seemed to be suspended in mid-air. They lowered themselves onto the smooth stone. From their perch, a spectacular view of the Black Mountains stretched for miles in every direction. Hickory, maple, oak and ash were beginning to ignite the surrounding ridges in a blaze of color.

"Look what I brought us." Julian reached into his backpack and pulled out a carefully wrapped cream cheese swirl brownie, Lily's favorite.

"That was so sweet of you," she said.

Julian divided it and passed half to Lily. "Sweets for the sweet," he said.

Lily took a bite. "Yum. This is the best."

They finished desert and rested at what seemed like

the edge of the world. After a while, the wind stilled. A solitary puff of cloud, like a triple-domed city, floated slowly across the sky, it's rim beginning to eclipse the sun. The landscape became bathed in violet-gold haze.

"It's magnificent, isn't it?" Julian said.

Lily smiled. It felt as if they were the last two people on earth.

After a few minutes, Julian heard Lily call him, not with a voice, but with an inside yearning. He turned toward her. An aura glowed around her as if she were made of light. To Lily, Julian, too, appeared luminous; serene and elegant as a god. Enveloped by a sense of peace they could not have imagined, exquisite pulsations began to vibrate within them, between them, around them, building in ecstatic intensity.

A short distance away, the vision of a man and a woman appeared. Dressed in the robes of monk and abbess, Lily and Julian immediately recognized them— Abelard, old and weary, shoulders stooped, hair silver-white and wiry beneath his skullcap; Heloise, shrouded in her habit, head lowered, her demeanor sad and forlorn. Although side by side, neither monk nor abbess seemed to notice the presence of the other, as if an invisible wall separated them.

Lily and Julian became mesmerized as their ancient counterparts glided toward them. The years now miraculously melted from their faces, their religious raiment returning to the ruffle and lace of lovers. They looked the way Lily had often imagined them in their youth—beautiful, vibrant, passionate. Abelard took Heloise's hand, brought it to his lips. They moved closer still, and Lily and Julian found themselves gazing into familiar eyes radiant with understanding and compassion.

As quickly as it had appeared, the vision spun itself into a trillion singing points of light and Lily and Julian were lifted into its music. In an instant, a thousand images of every soul expression they had ever been or ever will be flashed within their cells. A Lemurian architect. An Egyptian priestess. A Japanese rice farmer. A Grecian statesman. A Lady in Waiting to the Queen of Scotland. A Persian goat herder. A blind gravedigger. A painter. A poet. A concubine. A thief. A dream maker. A journey weaver. A Benedictine monk. A grieving abbess...

Then, in the vastness of an eternal moment, all thought vanished, all form became meaningless. Suddenly, there was no Lily, no Julian, no feminine, no masculine, no longer any separation. As one heart, they knew the all-encompassing, faceless face of love, and it was their own.

Seconds afterward, Lily and Julian were startled back into their bodies. It took several minutes for them to feel their way to ordinary consciousness.

"Lily, did you...?" Julian began, almost breathless, the flush of ecstasy still present in his voice.

"Yes," she whispered. Knowing they'd had the same experience was as amazing to Lily as *what* they'd experienced.

They looked around. The solitary plume of cloud they'd noticed before being swept away was just now completing its eclipse of the sun. A violet shadow widened over the landscape. From the lookout platform above them, they could hear several people marveling out loud at the view. Lily closed her eyes, trying to hold on to what was left of heaven. The wind had picked up and she felt chilled. Shivering, she pulled the hood of her sweatshirt over her head.

Locked again in physicality, Lily and Julian felt small and dense, their current reality dim, constricted and filled with inescapable limitation. There, they knew they each had to face where choice and circumstance had led them. Yet, they also knew they'd glimpsed something larger than the boundary of a body, or even a lifetime.

"It was incredible," Julian whispered.

They struggled to put into language what was beyond it.

"There was only...love." Lily began to weep. "It was *being* love, and I don't want it to go away."

"I know," Julian said through his own tears. "Neither do I."

"Look at us." Lily dug in her knapsack for a tissue.

Julian laughed softly, wiped his eyes with the back of his hand. For a few moments, they sat in silence.

"How could something so luminous be fading so fast?" Lily said.

Julian turned so he could see her face. He smoothed her cheek. "What it lit in us can never go out."

As if on some cosmic cue, the sun began to re-emerge, rolling back the blanket of shadow that had dimmed the landscape. Everything shimmered with new life.

Lily hooked her arm in Julian's. "Promise me that," she said. She knew it was too easy to lose truth in an illusionary world. Yet she also knew despite whatever sea of circumstance might seem to float between them, and no matter how many miles or centuries or light-years might appear to part them, as long as they remembered, there could be no separation. "Promise me you won't forget."

In an echo of Abelard's gesture, Julian took Lily's hand and gently kissed it. "I won't forget," he said. "I promise."

CHAPTER 23

...and then the day came when the risk
to remain tight in a bud was more painful
than the risk it took to blossom.

—Anaïs Nin

Winter wrapped itself luxuriously around Lily like cashmere. She spent her days at InWord Bound assisted by the perpetual cheerfulness of Maya. As she eased back into her center, she found renewed pleasure in the simple conversation with customers that she so enjoyed. For a while Lily and Julian communicated often. Perhaps because of their history, they both savored handwritten letters they could hold, pages that contained the imprint of the other. Lily sent Julian poems, told him about the novel she had started, asked him how he felt about seeing bits and pieces of himself—only the best ones of course—upon a page. Julian wrote about hibiscus as wide as the moon, the fragrance of ginger and plumeria. He sent Lily tiny dried ulu-ulu flowers from the rain forest, taught her the lovely Hawaiian word for hope, *mana'olana*, which literally meant floating thoughts.

The absence of winter, for Julian, was a welcome relief, and he delighted in the lushness of his life on Kauai. With distractions at a minimum, Julian's art flourished reflecting new confidence and freedom, and he was encouraged by his discoveries. He craved texture and applied his pigments with anything that would make them dimensionally alive—a knotted scrap of burlap, a wedge of natural sponge. Like Gauguin, he yearned for brilliant, sumptuous emerald and magenta, carmine, ochre and ultramarine, colors as luxuriant as the natural richness of his island paradise. Alone in his studio, Julian sometimes donned a brightly patterned lava lava, and placed a wreath of maile leaves a friend had made for him in his hair.

Yet in quiet moments, he still felt a profound loneliness—for Lily and for Sam. In Katherine's house, the memory of Sam was more immediate than it had been in Asheville. Yet, so was the void left by Lily, and during his first months there, Julian grieved his losses until his tears were as used up as a desert. But he also sighed in awe of having known love as deeply as he had—twice. In an unfeeling world it seemed a rare privilege.

For Lily, although Julian was no longer there in ordinary ways, his comforting, non-physical presence wove through her days. Sometimes she would sense him near her or even feel his face inside her own, the crease in his right cheek in hers as she smiled. Sometimes she would become aware of him in a flicker of firelight or the shimmer of rain. It was not the intrusive, emotionally shattering kind of sensation she had experienced in the past, but a gentle reminder that she was not alone.

Time and space soon healed the urgency in both of them, and Lily and Julian fell into a wider rhythm of communication. The letters between them became fewer and farther apart, yet even as they moved forward in their separate lives, they always felt the ever present love that transcended language.

One December evening, when an unexpected snowfall under a full moon turned everything fantastic, Lily sat by the window reflecting upon the extraordinary experiences of the past months. As she thought about Lovina and how much help she'd been, the phone rang. No longer surprised by Lovina's uncanny way of "appearing" right on cue, Lily suspected it was her.

"I'm glad you called," Lily said.

"I knew you would be." Lovina sounded her usual jovial self.

"I wanted to thank you," Lily continued.

"Thank yourself," Lovina said. "The choice was always yours. And the choice of choice is always love."

"Yes, I see that now."

Suddenly Lovina jolted the conversation in an unexpected direction. "So, have you spoken with David at all?"

"David?" It took a moment for Lily to make an association between the name, and the man she had met at Maya's birthday party back in September. "Oh, David." She felt a surprising tenderness stir with his memory. "No, I haven't."

"Well," Lovina said, "you might think about doing so."

I might, Lily thought. She knew that she'd grown beyond shutting down her heart, that she would love again. But for now, there was still much to contemplate.

In her journal she wrote:

Although nothing further is possible between me and Julian in the way I had hoped when I was dissolved in my misery, our relationship has given me more than I'd ever realized. At least, unlike Heloise, I was able to move beyond grieving an entire lifetime for the loss of a man who couldn't be what I'd imagined him to be. I can see now that Abelard had not been capable of the depth of love Heloise had felt for him, the kind of love she'd wanted to believe he'd felt for her. She was young and vulnerable, and may have trusted too much in Abelard's affections, believed too much that because she held a vision of the best of him, that was who he was. Women often think if they can only love a man enough, or in the right way, it will fix everything. Yet, it never does.

In my largest moments, I see that my time with Julian has taught me how to love unconditionally, reminded me how to be love. And it's showed me that passion, in its purest sense, is self-generated, and doesn't depend upon what another is or is not, or what he chooses to do or not to do. I've discovered that, given a seemingly impossible choice between having the person without the feeling, or the feeling without the person, in the deepest places of the spirit it is always the feeling we humans are after. It feels natural to love. It is what we are. And because Julian lives in my heart forever, he will always have my love—for doing nothing, for only being divinely who he is. And I know he gives the same to me. This is my comfort.

I'm beginning to understand many truths, even if I can't

always sustain the living of them. It seems to be a constant balancing act between humanity and divinity. Writing out of the best of me I am sounding very grand tonight. Yet I have moments when the less grand part, which still sits alone in this body by the fire, thinks of Julian and longs for a human touch, a sensual caress, a soft kiss.

Julian and I shared an opportunity for resolution and healing which we were both courageous enough to recognize. I wonder how many such gifts are sent back unopened because they're not neatly wrapped, or have knotted ribbons that require a steady patience to unwind.

Lily gazed out the window at the surreal landscape. Snow was falling softly, blanketing the hillside in pristine white. She thought about Julian, about how far they'd journeyed together. Loving him had brought out the best in her, inspired her to become more than she'd ever believed she could be. But in this life, Lily knew she and Julian must continue apart, fulfill their separate destinies. Yet she couldn't help wondering if, in some distant tomorrow, they might find their way to each other again.

As she set aside her journal, Lily became aware of Heloise hovering close. Although the disturbing dreams had long disappeared, on occasion Lily still felt her presence, but in a way far different from the tortured nun she had first encountered. She now sensed in her a deep serenity, as if all that Lily had lived reached through time to her counterpart, and Heloise, too, had gleaned its insight. Maybe, she thought, that was how it worked.

EPILOGUE

The story of Lily and Julian, in its largest sense, began very long ago with the true and tragic history of Abelard and Heloise. It was France, the 12th century. Peter Abelard was a brilliant, well-respected teacher, theologian and philosopher. An original thinker, his devoted students often traveled long distances to seek him out. He was in his mid-thirties, handsome and charming. He composed love songs.

Heloise, seventeen, had completed her studies at the convent at Argenteuil. Having no other family, she came to Paris to live with her uncle, Fulbert, a canon in the church. Her uncle loved her and had provided for her education.

Heloise possessed above average beauty and superior intelligence, and when Abelard met her he fell deeply under her spell. But celibacy was the custom for teachers, and so he felt he had a reputation to uphold. With the innocent help of some of Fulbert's friends, however, he connived to become a boarder in Fulbert's house. He then offered to tutor Heloise, and since her uncle had a weakness for both money and for nourishing his niece's intellect, he trusted in Abelard's good reputation.

Abelard and Heloise fell passionately in love and began an affair virtually under Fulbert's nose. With the pretense of lessons, they had no problem finding time to be alone together. And both being uninhibited in their passion, they took great pleasure in their love-making.

Completely absorbed in Heloise, Abelard soon became reckless in his outer behavior. He often neglected his students, ignored the gossip about him, and even allowed his love songs, which mentioned Heloise by name, to be sung in public. Miraculously, this went on for several months before Fulbert discovered their affair.

Fulbert was beside himself with shame and anger and feelings of betrayal. The lovers were beside themselves with the grief of their separation and concern for one another— Abelard for the shame that would be brought upon Heloise, Heloise with sorrow over Abelard's disgrace.

To complicate matters, within a short time, Heloise found she was pregnant. Despite everything, she was filled with joy. She asked Abelard what to do. Fulbert traveled often and while he was away, Abelard secretly sent Heloise to his sister's house in Brittany to wait for him. There she gave birth to their son, whom she named Astralabe.

When Fulbert returned and found out what had happened, he went wild with grief and mortification, but he knew he couldn't harm Abelard, or Abelard's family might take revenge upon Heloise. Pitying Fulbert, Abelard finally went to him and begged his forgiveness, even as he protested that in the eyes of love he had done nothing unusual. He offered to marry Heloise, but asked that it be kept secret, since teachers were expected not to marry. He didn't want to be forced to give up the brilliant career he'd managed to maintain.

Fulbert appeared to reconcile with him and agreed to secrecy. Abelard then left for Brittany to bring Heloise back and marry her, but he found that Heloise, strongly opposed to the marriage, argued passionately against it. She believed her uncle would *not* be appeased by any marriage, and that the world would ultimately punish her for ruining Abelard's reputation and snuffing out his light. She argued that Abelard had been created for all mankind, not to be bound to a single woman, that the name of mistress instead of wife was dearer to her and more honorable for Abelard. She said only love, freely given, and not the constriction of a marriage tie, should bind them to each other. But she couldn't dissuade Abelard and finally consented to marry him. Through her tears she exclaimed prophetically—"We shall both be destroyed. All that is left us is suffering as great as our love has been."

Abelard and Heloise returned to Paris, leaving their infant son with Abelard's sister. In the presence of Fulbert and some of his and their friends, Abelard and Heloise were married. Afterwards, with heavy hearts, they went their separate ways, only meeting when they could do so unobserved. Heloise's belief about her uncle, however, proved true. Soon Fulbert broke his promise of secrecy and had his servants spread the news of the marriage. When Heloise denied this to them, Fulbert turned against her, verbally shaming her and threatening to strike her. When Abelard heard of this, he sent Heloise to the convent at Argenteuil where she had been brought up. He had her disguise herself in the habit of a novice, so she would be safer while traveling.

Fulbert, however, imagined Abelard had tricked him and actually forced Heloise to become a nun, and what happened next marked the greatest tragedy of both their lives. In his rage, Fulbert arranged for his servants to sneak into Abelard's rooms in the middle of the night and castrate him. The next morning, when the news got out, the whole affair became a public as well as a private horror. It seemed the entire city gathered at Abelard's door, people—especially his students—weeping and wailing until Abelard felt more pain from shame and humiliation, than he did from his wound.

Eventually, believing no other options opened to them, Abelard thought it best that Heloise take religious vows, as he, too, did shortly afterwards. She became a nun, later an abbess, and he, a monk. They never saw each other again, except once, formally and very briefly, when Heloise and her nuns relocated to the monastery Abelard founded.

It was twelve years later that Heloise accidentally came across the long letter of consolation Abelard had written to a friend in which he described in detail the story of his own misfortunes. Moved to the depths of grief and longing, she felt compelled to begin a correspondence that has survived over eight hundred years, words that bear witness to both the anguish and the love left upon their souls, for nothing is ever lost.

ABOUT THE AUTHOR

Rachelle Rogers is a writer, poet, and author of *POSSOONS, stories*, and *Rare Atmosphere, a memoir*. She lives in Asheville, NC.

Visit her website at www.rachellerogers.com